Autumn of Amie

Book Seven of
The Guesthouse Girls Series

Judy Ann Koglin

Maui Shores Publishing

Kihei 2021

D1343145

Autumn of Emma Copyright © 2021 by Maui Shores Publishing

Kihei, HI 96753
http://www.mauishorespublishing.com

Unless otherwise indicated, Scripture quotations are from: *The Holy Bible*, American Standard Version (ASV)

Library of Congress Control Number: 2021905156

ISBN 978-1-953799-12-8 (paperback)
ISBN 978-1-953799-13-5 (e-book)

CHAPTER ONE

Aftermath of Tragedy

The air seemed gloomy when Amie woke up Sunday morning, her pillow wet from a nighttime of sobbing. She looked around her well-decorated pink and lavender room trying to figure out why she felt so horrible. Then, she remembered. She was hoping it was just a nightmare, but she knew it was real.

Too real.

Last night, four senior boys from her high school had been killed by a semi-truck while they were driving home from a victorious afternoon football game. Chelan was a small town in Washington State, and everyone who lived there pretty much knew everyone else, or they were at least connected to someone in their family in some way. Amie was a junior in high school and had grown up in Chelan and was only one grade behind the four boys who had been killed, so she knew all of them, to some degree.

One of them, Tanner, even worked part-time in the restaurant of her family's Lakeside Resort. She thought about him. He always had a ready smile and something adventurous to do. He loved all sports, but he lived for football. He was a running back, and he was so excited for summer to come to a conclusion so that his senior season of football games would start. She couldn't believe he was dead. *That means that yesterday was the last game he would ever play*, she thought.

Then, her mind turned to Tyson, Tanner's best friend. Amie smiled remembering his red hair that always seemed past-due for a haircut, and his ever-present grin. Tyson was also a running back on the football team, and he and Tanner took turns running the plays in to the rest of the team. Amie knew that he had just started dating Kari, a senior girl, recently, and they always looked happy together. They were a cute couple. She must be devastated.

She didn't know dark-haired Bryan or light-blond John as well as the other two boys, but she knew that Bryan was in a serious relationship with a girl on the soccer team.

Amie's heart ached. She spent some time still in bed thinking of every memory she had of working with Tanner or hanging out with him and Tyson. She looked at her clock. Seven in the morning. Too early to call, but not too early to text Josh.

2

Josh was one of her coworkers from the resort whom she had grown close with lately. Although they hadn't gone on an official date yet, Amie really liked him. He had graduated from Chelan High in the spring and was leaving for college at the University of Washington next weekend. Josh had been good friends with Tanner and friends with the other boys, too, and Amie wondered how he was doing. She hesitated to text in case the alert woke him up. She wasn't sure how much sleep he had gotten last night. She took the risk anyway, deciding that, if he was exhausted, he would probably sleep through the alert.

"Hey, Josh, just checking to see how you were doing?" Amy typed.

His reply came at lightning speed: "Not feeling so great this morning. I still can't believe it happened. 4 great guys. 4 seniors. Crazy."

"I know. Crazy. R u going 2 church?" Amie replied.

"Yeah, I guess. Everyone will probably be there today."

"Yeah. Do you work today?" Amie asked.

"No, do you?" Josh's reply read.

"Yes. Front desk for a while." Amie typed back.

"K."

Amie wished she had something more intelligent or appropriate to say, but she was still so shell-shocked by the news of the accident, she just sat there trying to guess what words would comfort him.

Finally, she typed, "C ya at church."

He sent her a checkmark emoji to end the conversation.

Amie thought about trying to sleep a little more, but she forced herself to get up and shower, blow dry her blonde bob with a medium-sized round brush, and figure out the right outfit for today. She wanted it to be plain and classic to reflect the solemn mood that everyone would be feeling. She chose a navy skirt and navy pumps with an ivory blouse. Labor Day had come and gone, so white was out of the question for now. *Who makes these stupid fashion rules?* she thought, *I love wearing white, and it is lame that you only can wear it for three months a year.* She dutifully buttoned up the ivory blouse and looked in the mirror. *That will work.* She went into the bathroom and put on her makeup. Her eyes still looked swollen and red from crying. She made sure she wore her waterproof mascara, even though she was pretty sure she was done crying, and she went to the kitchen for breakfast.

Amie lived in a large, picturesque house that had a panoramic view of Lake Chelan. There were windows in almost every room that had a view of the lake. Amie was excited to be back in the house because her parents had rented it out to another family this past summer while they were in Montana caring for Grandpa Peterson's back injury. While her family was out of state, Amie was able to stay in Chelan for the summer because her parents booked her a room in The Guesthouse under the watchful care of a sweet lady from their church named Aunty Nola. Amie loved her summer at The Guesthouse and loved her three roommates: Hope, Emma, and Kendi. All three of them had come to Chelan from various cities to cover the demand for summer workers during the heavy tourist season. Hope actually got to remain in Chelan at the end of the summer and start school at Chelan High, and Amie was happy to be able to keep one of her new friends in town with her. Emma and Kendi had returned to their homes in Pasco and Redmond, but they had promised to keep in touch. Amie had texted Emma and Kendi last night to tell them what happened since they also knew some of the boys from social events this past summer.

Amie's mom and dad were just finishing bowls of granola cereal, and Amie went to the cupboard and got some for herself. She poured the almond milk on the granola and silently enjoyed the vanilla flavor and the crunchy texture of the cereal.

Her mom looked at her. "How ya doing, Amie?"

"I'm ok, just really sad. I can't believe it happened."

"I know, it is surreal," her dad, Randy, agreed. "I'm sure church will be packed today because people are just going to want to be together and talk."

"I think so, too," Staci agreed. "We better get going as soon as Amie finishes her breakfast."

"I'm finished," Amie replied, carrying her mostly-empty bowl to the sink, rinsing it out, and putting it in the dishwasher.

"Okay. Let's go," Staci urged, holding open the door to their garage.

****

They drove the mile and a half to church, and when they arrived, Amie hurried out of the car and looked for Josh in the lobby. He was easy to locate because he was a tall guy with light blond hair and a golden tan. Their eyes met, and she went over to him and gave him a hug. Amie could tell that he seemed relieved to see her.

"Do you want to go sit?" he asked.

"Sure," Amie replied.

"Do you mind sitting with my parents? My mom is freaked out that I'm leaving for college next weekend. She thinks it is the last time I will sit with her in church," he joked. Then, he paused, thinking of Tanner and the other boys. "I'm sorry ... I guess that was in poor taste."

"Don't worry about it," Amie advised. "Let's go sit with your parents. I totally get why she would want to spend this time with you before you leave."

They got seated, and soon, church started.

Pastor James addressed what everyone was already thinking about: the accident. He said that he didn't change his sermon because the one he had planned to give today was spot on given the tragedy that had happened. He personally knew all four of the boys because Tanner and Tyson went to church there regularly, and Bryan and John had attended occasionally. He knew that God had planned this message because what happened yesterday was not a surprise to God. The pastor went on to preach a sermon that talked about how Jesus was omnipresent, which meant that He was with us every day of our lives, and on the last day of our time on earth, he would be there to welcome us into Heaven, if we had chosen to accept His gift of salvation. He mentioned that a lot of times people think they get a free pass to heaven because they think they are basically a good person.

Pastor James said, "Our salvation has nothing to do with how good we are, but it has everything to do with how good He is. We sin every day, and that sin is enough to keep us separated from God and eternal life in Heaven." He went on to talk about how Jesus is there for us as we mourn this tragedy, and that there were people at the altar if anyone wanted someone to pray with. Amie was glad to know that she had accepted Jesus when she was a little girl, and that she knew she would get to see Jesus someday, as well as loved ones she had lost along the way. She breathed a silent prayer that this tragedy would draw people to Jesus, so the boys' deaths would not be in vain.

After church, Josh and Amie went to the lobby. Pretty soon, Amie's friend Hope, whom she had met at The Guesthouse this summer, joined them.

Hope asked Josh how he was doing.

"I can't believe it is real." Josh answered. "We were just together yesterday morning before the guys left for the game, and we worked the same shift last Saturday. He was a great guy, kind of mischievous, and always fun!"

"The other guys were great, too," Amie took up the conversation. "I've known them forever. The school will not be the same this year. I feel so badly for their families."

"Me, too," Hope agreed sadly. "Such a tragedy."

"It sounds like a bunch of people are meeting at the school gym this afternoon. They are opening it up so friends can have a place to gather." Amie mentioned.

As she was speaking, Ben, a mutual friend, walked up to the group. Ben was tall with blue eyes and blond hair with the look of a surfer. He nodded to Amie and Hope, and he leaned in and hugged Josh. "How you doing, man?" he asked.

"Not great," Josh admitted, "but I heard you were first on the scene. How are *you* doing?"

Ben said that he and a couple of his friends were driving the car right behind the one that was in the accident yesterday and saw the smashed car with his own eyes. He shared with them some of the details, including the heartbreak the semi-truck driver who had accidentally swerved into the wrong lane and caused the fatal collision, experienced. "The semi truck driver was devastated," Ben said.

"Oh my gosh, I'm so sorry, Ben," Amie murmured, and Hope nodded sadly.

"That must have been awful, man," Josh sympathized. As he was speaking, Ben's parents, Mark and Rachel Brandon, owners of the local coffee shop, joined the group, accompanied by Josh's parents.

After greeting the others and exchanging a few comments, Rachel asked, "Ready to go, Ben?"

"Yeah, I need to have some downtime, I think. Who is working at the shop?" The Brandons owned the local coffee shop and bakery.

"Lynn is working today. She is going to keep it open later today if there are people who need to hang out. Some people are gathering at the gym so she may not need to stay late."

Ben then turned to Josh. "When do you leave for school, buddy?"

"I'll leave next weekend. Classes start after that."

"Well, in case I don't see you, have a great semester."

"Thanks, Ben, but you'll see me. I am coming back sometimes on weekends to work at the resort and see friends," Josh replied with a meaningful glance toward Amie that sent a small shiver of excitement down her spine.

Ben smiled, and the Brandons said goodbye to everyone. Josh's parents nodded goodbye and headed in the same direction.

Amie saw that her parents were getting their jackets on, so she gave Hope and Josh each a hug, then whispered to Josh, "I'm off at five if you want to talk."

Josh nodded, and Amie left to join her parents, who were heading toward the door. She and her dad were both working at the resort today, so the three of them were going to get sandwiches at Beaches, the lunch counter at the resort, before Amie's shift started.

****

While they were eating, they discussed the situation that was on everybody's mind.

"How ya doing, Amie?" her dad asked.

"I'm doing okay. To be honest, I wasn't super close to any of the boys, but I knew all of them. This will leave a huge hole in the senior class. And I feel so sorry for their families and their friends and girlfriends."

"Me, too," her mom agreed. "I am so upset for all the parents. It makes me never want to let you out of my sight!"

"Well, I have to start work now, so unless you want to sit in the lobby all day, I'm going to be out of your sight…but I'll be just fine," Amie teased, getting up and giving her mom a kiss on the cheek. "See ya guys later. Mom, are you picking us up at five?"

"Yep. I'm going over to Aunty Nola's with some of the other ladies, and we are going to talk about what we can do to help the four families. I'll be back at five. See you both then!"

Amie and her dad walked down the stairs to the lobby, and her dad gave her a side hug and a wave as he pushed open the door and walked across to the building where the maintenance office was located.

Amie stepped behind the front desk where her aunt, Debbie was working with a lady named Linda. Amie's aunt, together with Amie's uncle, Bob, managed the operations of the resort. Amie's dad Randy was the maintenance manager, and her mom Staci, a CPA, handled the resort's finances from her home office.

"Hi, Amie! I'm glad you're here. Bob and I are going to take off. We are going over to visit Tanner's family. I don't think we'll be back today, but call if you need us."

After Linda and Amie assured Debbie that they would be fine, Debbie grabbed her brown purse and her keys and met her husband out front at their car.

There was a fairly steady stream of calls to the front desk for restaurant advice, questions about the nearby area, help with unlocking their safe, and other typical queries. During the slow times, Linda and Amie discussed the tragedy. Linda was friends with John's mom and knew that she was devastated, as were the other parents.

"Should you be with John's mom now?" Amie asked.

"I was last night," Linda explained. "She had family come in this morning, so she has a house full. They are well-supported, so I felt okay with coming into work."

A few new guests arrived at the resort early, and, because there were some vacancies, Amie was able to offer them early check-ins.

By three o'clock, the lobby started filling up with guests ready to check in. Linda and Amie greeted everyone with smiles, processed them as quickly as they could, and directed them to their rooms. The weather was still nice, but it was taking on a decidedly more fall appearance in the last week. Amie was a summer girl through and through, but she did enjoy watching the leaves change colors and dance across the ground, and she was excited for the changing of the seasons. One of her favorite parts of autumn was the apple harvest that would be happening in about a month. Amie and her parents did u-picking in the orchard behind Aunty Nola's Guesthouse and brought home several varieties of apples, which they made into pies, strudels, and applesauce.

Chelan was a lakeside town, and the resort was booked solid during the summer and fairly well during the winter ski season, but spring and fall were much less busy. It was getting close to the time when there would be fewer check-ins, and Amie knew that the hours would drop for employees. She was okay with not working for awhile because she had plenty to do at school, and other people who were supporting families needed to get their hours in more than she did.

Linda jolted her out of her thoughts. "How's Josh doing? I know he was friends with Tanner."

"Yes, he was, and he is pretty devastated – we all are. He was glad that he had today off work because he didn't think he could handle working in Beaches today, especially since he and Tanner worked a shift together last week."

"This is going to be a tough loss for the whole town, but we'll get through it together. That is the great thing about living in a small town. We are always there for each other."

"True," Amie agreed. "My mom is working with Nola to see what kind of assistance would be most wanted by the families. So many people want to contribute. Even the girls who lived at The Guesthouse with me this summer were asking about how their families could help."

Just then, at the same time, the front desk phone rang, and another check-in arrived. Linda and Amie had plenty to do before Amie left for the day.

****

When she was in the car with her parents after work, her mom updated them on what was decided at Aunty Nola's place. They were going to hold the memorial service for the four boys together at the football stadium, and it was going to be huge. They would likely be putting together a memorial fund of some sort, but the details would be decided in the coming days.

When they were pulling into their garage, Amie received a call from Kendi, who was hoping for some more information about the accident. Amie explained some of the info about the boys, and the plans to try to keep the football season going if they could.

"What about the funeral?" Kendi asked.

"It will be a Celebration of Life for the four boys, and they are going to do it as a group at the football stadium next Saturday. It is going to be huge because all the families are well-known.

"My mom was wondering if there was anything she could do for the families?" Kendi asked.

"My mom was wondering that, too. We'll let you know when they figure something out," Amie assured.

Kendi encouraged her friend to hang in there.

"Thank you for being a good friend," Amie replied.

The girls said goodbye and hung up. By the time the call ended, Amie was settled in her room wearing stylish sweatpants and a matching jacket.

Her phone rang again. This time, it was Josh. They spent the next hour talking. Josh shared with Amie about how he would probably leave on Saturday after the service, so he could have time to get settled into his dorm before classes started. He was excited to meet his roommate, a guy from California who was planning to major in chemical engineering.

"Are you excited to get started with college?" Amie asked.

"Yes, but every time I start to feel excited, I feel guilty because of Tanner. He won't ever get to go off to college. He won't even be able to finish high school. He was larger than life, and everyone loved him. It is hard to be happy about anything right now with all that is going on here."

"I understand," Amie agreed, "but remember, you're not being disloyal to them just because you are enjoying your college experience. If the tables were turned, you'd probably want them to do the same, I would imagine."

"Yeah, that's probably true," Josh reflected. "I probably would want them to go to my celebration of life and say something nice about me, then move on with their lives."

"Exactly!" Amie agreed, "and that is just what you are planning to do. So don't worry." Amie and Josh could both hear Amie's mom calling her for dinner. Amie could smell the tantalizing fragrance of ginger chicken stir-fry, one of her mom's specialties.

"Guess you gotta go," Josh remarked.

"Yeah, but hopefully, I'll see you before you go."

"Count on it!" Josh replied. "Have a good night, Amie!"

"Bye!" Amie said. She hit the red icon on her phone to disconnect the call and leaned back on her bed with a happy sigh. She indulged in a moment of reliving the phone conversation with Josh before she heard her mom calling her for dinner again.

"Coming!" Amie called back. She scurried down the tan carpeted stairs and slid on the shiny wood floor of the entry way with her socks. She landed right in front of one of the dining room chairs and plopped down.

"That was quite an entrance," her dad commented.

"Yep!" Amie replied happily.

"You look happy! Who were you just talking to?" her mom asked.

Amie tried to appear nonchalant. "Just one of my co-workers, Josh."

"Hmmm—Josh again? I'm beginning to see a pattern," her dad joked.

"Well, not much of a pattern because he's leaving for U-dub after the Celebration of Life on Saturday," Amie mentioned.

"Oh, good, I guess we dodged a bullet on that one."

"What do you mean? Josh is great!" Amie argued.

"I'm sure he is. He'll just be a great guy in the U-District," her dad commented. "The University of

17

Washington might have some good academic programs but I'll take a WSU Cougar anytime for my girl."

"Okay, dad, I'll keep that in mind," Amie assured him. Amie dug into the fragrant chicken-ginger stir-fry that was getting cold. "So, Dad, about me driving…"

"Yes, we discussed it, and you can start borrowing your mom's car to take to school when she doesn't need it. We'll look for a cheap little car for you, too."

She finished her dinner, cleared the table, and put the leftovers in plastic containers and put them in the fridge. She took a yellow and white dishcloth and happily wiped down the oak table and dried it with a towel. She carefully hung both the dishcloth and towel on the oven handle and went upstairs to her room to get ahead on her homework, although she knew she wouldn't have class for the next two days.

She was finally going to drive, and that was totally great news!

When Amie settled into her room, she picked up her cell and noticed she had missed a call from Ryan. She hit the redial button.

"Hi, Ryan! I hope I'm not calling too late."

"Oh, hi, Amie. Mr. Wilson just called me and told me that they were going to have grief counselors at the school tomorrow and Tuesday."

"Wow. I've never heard of the principal calling someone at home," Amie remarked.

"Well, he called because he didn't think kids would want to go to grief counselors since they might think they don't need any help, or that if they went, other kids would think they were weak or something. He asked me if I could visit a grief counselor and encourage some of my friends who have some influence to do the same, so we could help eliminate the stigma. There is a calendar on the school's website, and we can make an appointment there. After our session, we can tell other students about it to whatever extent we want, or make a post on social media. The administration wants all the students to get useful tools to help everyone process their grief, I guess. So, I thought about someone who would be influential in the junior class, and your name kept coming to mind. You're the junior class president, aren't you?"

"Secretary, actually. Thanks for thinking of me. I don't see myself as an influencer, but I am glad to make an appointment on the calendar and post about it, I guess."

"Okay. Thanks, Amie. Who do you think would be good in the younger grades?"

"Probably people who actually knew the boys who were in the accident. Maybe JV football players?"

"Yeah, I was thinking that, too. I'll text some of them and see if we can get some appointments filled."

"Okay! Good luck!" Amie replied, then they said goodbye and hung up.

Amie looked up the school's website, clicked on the grief counselor appointment link, and put herself down for a ten o'clock appointment. She didn't want to get up too early since it was a day off from school.

Amie called her friend Hannah and relayed the message that Ryan had given her.

"I guess I could go. It might be awkward, though," Hannah replied. "Do you want to go together?"

"Sure, if they let us. I have an appointment for ten o'clock tomorrow morning if you want to come." Amie knew that about a year ago, Hannah had dated John, one of the boys who had been killed in the accident, for a couple months. They had broken up, rather spectacularly, over a misunderstanding. However, once they had cleared up the issue, they were still both too stubborn to get back together. Eventually, they had both moved on, but Hannah told Amie that there was still some regret that she thought she could talk about with the counselors.

"Are you sure you want me there?" Amie asked.

"Oh, yeah. I would feel more comfortable with you there. You already know the whole story between me and John. We haven't talked in months, but I can't believe he's gone," Hannah replied with a sigh.

"I know," Amie agreed soothingly. "I'll see you tomorrow morning."

****

Amie drove to school the next day and spent some time hanging out at the school gym with her friends Lexi, a medium height girl of Korean ancestry, Amanda, a cheerful girl with thick brown hair with bangs, and green-eyed, blonde Hailey. At 9:45, Hannah walked into the gym, still looking sleepy. Amie explained to the other girls that she and Hannah were going to talk to a grief counselor, and she would let them know how it went after their appointment.

The counseling appointment turned out to be good. It mostly involved Hannah processing her grief about John. That was okay with Amie because she didn't have anything specific in her life to talk about.

Afterwards, they encouraged the other girls to make appointments since the counselor was so helpful. Hailey wasn't interested, but Amanda wanted to do it, and Lexi agreed to go with her for moral support.

Amie felt like the time sitting around the school gym was pretty odd. Many of the kids who were there were underclassmen who didn't even know the seniors who were in the accident, so they were just there to socialize.

Amie wished they would just go somewhere else. The people who were the hardest hit by grief, such as the families of the boys in the accident and their close friends, mainly hung out at their own homes and didn't venture out to the school. Amie thought that was just as well because the atmosphere in the gym didn't seem too great with all the underclassmen milling around.

Amie hung out a little longer and saw Ben and Ryan and some of their other friends go to their grief counselor appointments and come out.

Amie asked Ryan how it went.

"I think it was really good," said Ryan. "It gave me a chance to talk about the guys to someone who didn't know them, so I really learned how to describe each of them, talk about how I felt about them, and how I miss them. I think it was good. I think everyone who had a relationship with one of them should really try it."

"Me, too," Amie agreed. "Oh, I forgot to post about it. I'll do that now." Amie made some quick keystrokes on her phone, and a social media post was up within the minute across a number of platforms.

"Hey, me and Ben and some of the guys are going to play some hoops outside, so I'll see ya later, Amie."

****

Amie nodded and waved. "Okay! Bye!"

On Tuesday, Amie didn't bother to go to the school, but later in the afternoon, Josh texted to see if she wanted to go for a walk. She was thrilled that he asked, both because she had a mega-crush on him, but also, she wanted to be there for him because she knew he was grieving. After receiving permission from her mom, she borrowed her car and drove to the resort parking lot, met him when he got off his shift, and they took a walk on the beach path.

They didn't have a lot to say, but they made small talk about the pros and cons of working in Stillwaters, the fancier restaurant at the resort, versus Beaches, the casual lunch counter. She also told him about a hot, sweaty day she had that summer working in the resort's laundry room.

"Now, *those* ladies earn their money," Amie announced, hoping to put a smile on his troubled, but still really handsome face.

"I guess so!" he agreed, with a grin. "I'm glad I get to work at Beaches!"

After they talked awhile, they walked back to their respective cars, said goodbye, and went home.

Judy Ann Koglin

CHAPTER TWO

Learning and Growing

Amie was relieved to be back in school on Wednesday, so things could start to get back to normal. The teachers were going really easy on the homework this week, and Amie was glad about that.

Amie sat by Hope in Spanish class, and they chatted briefly. They decided to meet for lunch on Saturday to catch up. She was already looking forward to spending extra time with Hope, even though Saturday was three days from now.

Amie had heard that Aunty Nola was coordinating the food effort for after the Celebration of Life service on Saturday, so after school, she had arranged to stop by The Guesthouse to see if she could help with anything.

Amie drove to The Guesthouse in her mom's car, thrilled to finally have this privilege. Even though she lived there all summer, this was the first time she actually drove into the familiar circular driveway. She put the car in park, plucked her keys from the ignition, and went in, proudly jingling the keys that were dangling from her manicured hand. She had abandoned her typical pink nail color and chosen a forest green color, partially a nod to the impending autumn and as a reflection of the gravity of the week.

The keys were not lost on Aunty Nola. As she opened the door and gave Amie a big hug, she exclaimed, "Looks like someone got her driving privileges!"

"Yes!" Amie breathed a sigh of relief. "And it feels great!" Amie then sniffed the air. "What is that amazing fragrance?" She walked over to the stove where two large stockpots, both filled with yellowish liquid bubbling merrily.

"Chicken noodle soup," Aunty Nola revealed proudly. "I am filling mason jars for each family, so they will have some on hand if they need it."

"Do you have cookies in the oven, too?" Amie couldn't help but ask.

"Yes! Chocolate chunk," Nola confirmed.

"Oh, the best!" Amie squealed. "They'll love them!"

"Well, sit down, Sweetie, and we can talk about the food for the celebration of life."

Aunty Nola briefed her on the catering and the setup plans for the outdoor reception after Saturday's event. She also explained the plans for a memorial scholarship endowment they were setting up for future Chelan High football players.

"We've already collected a fairly large fund, so the earnings will help students for years to come," said Aunty Nola.

"What about the other expenses?" Amie asked.

"Two of the families were a little tight on money, so they received donations for the burial and headstones. The other families declined the contribution and preferred the money go toward the scholarship endowment. I think they are going to use their boys' college funds to pay for their burial. If that isn't the saddest thing …" She paused and wiped her eye. "The celebration of life will be funded by donations from business owners and other caring families."

Amie looked at Aunty Nola with admiration. "Looks like you got everything under control. How can I help?"

"How much time do you have?" Aunty Nola asked.

"As long as you need me. I have Youth Group tonight at seven, but I can skip it if you need me."

"No, don't miss that. It is important both for you and for the people you encourage when you are there."

"What do you mean?" asked Amie.

"Think about it this way: the youth pastor and his helpers work really hard to have fun games planned and a good message and music, only to have just a few kids bother to come."

"Well, they didn't waste their time, because someone showed up," Amie declared.

"Yes, but what if the next week fewer came because not many people came, and eventually, no one came? Whenever you show up and you bring your irresistible light with you, you are an encouragement to the leadership as well as the other kids who attend."

"I never looked at it like that," Amie contemplated. "So, in a way, I am serving just by showing up if I come with a good attitude."

"Yes ma'am. My husband Garry and I helped with the youth, and whenever we had students who we could count on showing up week after week and inviting their friends, we were so encouraged by them. Those students really helped our ministry. I remember we had a girl one time for whom Youth Group was her only social activity, so she was committed to making each meeting great. She took it upon herself to call everyone in the group each Wednesday afternoon to remind them about Youth Group encourage them to come. We were so blessed by her efforts."

"Wow! Do you still keep in touch with her?"

"Oh, yes. She is still really organized. In fact, she manages a big resort now."

Amie did a double take. "Do you mean my aunt Debbie?"

"One and the same," Aunty Nola replied, laughing.

"What a great story! It makes me never want to skip Youth Group again!"

"I hope you don't!" Aunty Nola agreed. "Now, how would you like to help me package up the cookies and chicken soup and deliver them to the families?"

"I would love it!" Amie replied and meant it.

They spent the next hour getting things packaged up and delivering it to the families. Each family accepted the boxes with grateful hearts and thanked Amie and Aunty Nola profusely.

When they got back to The Guesthouse, it was almost time for Amie to head to Youth Group. She had already texted her mom to let her know what she was doing, so Aunty Nola suggested she stay for some of the leftover soup and cookies before she had to leave for church.

Amie enjoyed the soup and cookies, and she took a few of the latter to share with her parents.

After dinner, she drove to Youth Group with a new attitude. She now considered herself sort of a student leader, and she was determined to make each student feel welcome and the leaders to feel appreciated and encouraged. Amie walked around, interacting with others and making sure no one felt left out.

She was wondering where Ben and Ryan were. They were usually the friendliest people in the group. Lexi told her that she had heard that they, along with their mutual friend Cody, had agreed to join the football team to help keep the season going. The team was holding extra practices, so the boys would be ready to play next week in Granger. Some people were wondering how they'd do since they hadn't played football in years, but some students were optimistic because the new additions were naturally athletic, even if they didn't have experience.

The talk that the youth pastor gave was good, and Amie thanked each leader at the end of the night. She felt like this was her favorite night at Youth Group in a while, and she was happy that she was now following the example set by her aunt over twenty years ago.

****

On Thursday night, Josh texted and asked her if she wanted to go on a walk. She checked with her mom who said it was okay. Once she got the green light, Amie hopped into the car and met him at the resort.

As they walked, Amie realized how agitated Josh was. They sat down on a bench, and she courageously asked him questions to help him figure out the source of his stress. Work was fine, and he was starting to process the fact that Tanner and the other guys were gone. He was still upset about the accident, but he didn't think that was the cause of his concern.

"Are you nervous about your roommate at UW or your classes?" Amie asked.

"No, not specifically, but I think this all has to do with leaving."

"What about your mom and her health?" she asked.

Amie remembered the night last summer when Josh received a call that his mom had to be rushed to the hospital in Wenatchee. Amie had dropped everything to be with him. The doctors had thought that she was having a recurrence of some issues from her cancer treatments, but they were able to get everything under control. Amie was happy she had been there for Josh that night and that she had the opportunity to meet Josh's dad and brother. She wondered passively what they would think of her spending this much time with him.

"I think that's it, Amie. I think I am scared that something will happen to my mom, and I won't be there for her. I don't want that."

"Oh, Josh, that is so commendable. But she doesn't feel like that, right?"

"No, she wants me to go and experience college life."

"And her health is okay now?"

"Yes, I think so."

"Does your dad want you to go?"

"Yes."

"I think what we need to do is pray for you to have peace about going off to college. You know you are only a few hours away, and you can drop everything and come back if you are needed."

"I know," he mumbled.

"How 'bout if I pray for you right now?" Amie asked a little nervously.

"Okay," Josh replied, his hesitancy indicating that he was feeling a little awkward.

Amie thought she should put a hand on his shoulder or something, but she decided just to fold her hands, so she wouldn't make the situation uncomfortable for the two of them. She said a quick prayer acknowledging that God was the Prince of Peace, and she asked Him to fill Josh with His peace since he was facing a lot of stress due to the death of his friends, starting college, and leaving his potentially sick mom. She asked the Holy Spirit to wash over Josh, sweep his anxiety away, and replace it with the peace that only He can give. Finally, she asked God to remind Josh to cast his burdens on Jesus, "just like You tell us to do in the Bible." She closed with, "In Jesus' name, amen."

Josh agreed, "Amen!" Then, he said, "Wow – you can pray, girl! You must do that a lot."

"I do pray a lot," Amie admitted, "but I probably should pray more. God always takes care of me, and I am always grateful to Him."

"Well – thanks! I guess we should get back."

"Yeah," Amie replied, and the two walked back in relative silence, each lost in their own thoughts.

When they reached their cars, Josh spoke. "You know I like you Amie, obviously. You're the one I've turned to all week... really, all summer. You're smart and pretty. Do you want to be my girlfriend?"

Amie's heart was fluttering all over the place at this point. But, for some reason, she held back. "Well, I like you too, Josh," she said, "and I do want to be your girlfriend, but maybe we should go on some official dates before we commit to a relationship." She laughed, hoping he wouldn't be put off too much with her response.

He laughed, too. "Oh, yeah, I guess I am putting the cart before the horse. Okay, I'm leaving this weekend, but I'll be back next weekend, and maybe we can go on an official date then."

"That would be great," Amie agreed. "I'd better get home now."

They said goodbye and got in their cars and drove home. As Amie drove, she couldn't help have a smile on her face after the compliments Josh gave her. *Smart and pretty. The one I've turned to all week and really, all summer.* She reiterated Josh's phrases in her mind and they warmed her heart. She loved the idea of dating tall, handsome Josh. However, he was leaving for UW in a couple days. *Could we make a long-distance relationship work?* she asked herself.

When she got home, he sent her a text that said, "Thanks for the prayer. I feel better."

She responded with a smiley face emoji.

****

Amie had hoped that Josh would ask her on a date for Friday night since he was leaving on Saturday. But on Thursday, he texted Amie and said that his brother was coming to town, and they were going to have a game night since it was the last night together before they took Josh to Seattle and moved him into his dorm.

Amie bit her lip in disappointment. She understood that his family would miss him and wanted to be with him, but so did she.

She texted Hannah: "R u busy 2nt?" She texted in shorthand since she wanted to make plans as soon as possible.

"Ya, Evan is in town and we r hanging out. U need anything?"

"No – we can hang another time."

"KK."

Amie texted her friend Hailey next: "R u busy 2nt?"

"No, why?"
"I thought we could get ice cream or something."

"Mmm, I'm on keto, so no ice cream, but maybe movies?"

"Sure! Text me if something looks good."

A few minutes later, Hailey texted back: "I've already seen the movies there so let's skip it."

Not to be deterred, Amie texted her friend Lexi: "What r u doing 2nt?"

"I'm in SEA for the weekend."

"Oh, ur missing the service tmrw?"

"Ya – Invited Students Day at Seattle U. There is a sclrshp contest I couldn't miss. Visiting UW tmrw 2."

"Ok, good luck in contest!"

"Thx – bye!"

Lexi was a gifted musician so Amie assumed her scholarship contest was a piano audition.

Amie went down to the kitchen and spoke to her mom, Staci. "Well, strike three. I guess I'm staying home," she lamented.

"What do you mean by 'strike three?'" Staci asked with interest.

"Heather is busy, Hailey is on keto, and Lexi is out of town."

"Hmmm, what about Josh? Doesn't he leave for college tomorrow?

Amie stared at her mom. *How does she know about Josh?*

"Well, you've been going for walks with him all week, so I thought you would be going on a date tonight."

"Me too, but his parents wanted to spend the last night before they left for college as a family." Amie pouted.

"Are you and Josh an item now?"

"Not exactly."

"Well, he seems like a nice boy. I just don't want to see you get your heart broken."

"MOM! It's not like that. We are friends from work. I am not going to get my heart broken! *Please!*" Amie wasn't ready to share her thoughts about Josh with her mom yet so she was hoping she would just drop the subject. Apparently, her protest was a little stronger than what she had intended.

"Careful, Amie-girl. It's that kind of attitude that caused you to lose your driving privileges this spring."

Amie remembered that as soon as the snarky words had come out of her mouth. "Sorry, Mom!" she blurted.

"Well, your dad and I were thinking of going to the movies tonight. There is one of those superhero movies that Dad likes out now, I forgot which one. If you could stand being seen with your parents, we would love to have you come with us."

Amie considered it, but said, "I don't want to encroach on your date night."

"Don't worry about that. We had all summer to have date nights when we were in Montana. We love to spend time with you."

Her dad, Randy, walked into the kitchen from the garage, saying, "What did we do in Montana?"

"We went on dates," Staci laughed.

"We did!" he confirmed, smiling at his wife.

"I guess I'm crashing your date," Amie revealed.

"Oh, awesome!" Randy enthused. "Your mom doesn't follow the superhero universe, so it will be good to have another person to explain things to her."

Staci laughed. "Maybe I have a few too many things going on in the real world to spend much time learning about a fake universe. That's what I have you guys for."

Randy looked at the microwave and noticed the time. "Hey, ladies, we better get moving if we are going to have time to buy snacks *and* see the trailers before it starts!"

"Okay! Let me get a sweater," Amie said before dashing up the stairs and returning with a cute dark blue cardigan that looked great with her cuffed, faded Capri-length jeans and stretchy, ivory v-neck top.

The three of them went through the garage door to the car and spent a fun evening watching the movie and debating its merits afterwards. Amie had a good time, and the evening was a good reminder about what cool parents she had.

CHAPTER THREE

Celebration of Life

Saturday had arrived. Amie got up early for her breakfast shift at the resort. She didn't usually work in the restaurant, but she wondered if she was replacing a shift that Tanner would have worked. She shuddered a little at the thought.

Amie was excited because she and Hope were going to meet at the sandwich shop when she got off work. When her shift ended, she dashed out to the parking lot and hustled to meet her friend. Hope had already arrived first and had found a table by the window in the far corner. Amie drove into the parking lot a few minutes later. She greeted Hope with a smile and hug.

Hope grinned. "It's so weird to see you driving."

"It has been a long time coming, but I am glad to finally be able to drive."

"I'm getting my license when my mom gets to town."

39

"Oh, how's that going?"

"Good. She comes to town almost every weekend to train at the store. She is really excited to live here permanently."

The girls chatted for awhile about how Hope was adjusting to living in Chelan and how much she loved her soccer team.

"But my big news is … I became a Christian!"

"REALLY?!" Amie squealed so loudly that the people in the other booths turned around to look. "I'm so happy! Let's order, and you can tell me all about it."

They ordered and then Hope told her how everything had unfolded. Amie loved every minute of the story. She had been praying that Hope would overcome any obstacle that was preventing her from accepting Jesus, and it looked like her prayers were answered.

"Do you want to start coming to my Bible study?" Amie asked. "We meet Sunday nights.

"I would love that," Hope replied.

"Okay! I'll text you the deets."

While they were devouring their sandwiches, Amie commented, "Josh has been having a rough week. He was good friends with Tanner, and he is taking it really hard."

"Oh, that is rough," Hope sympathized.

"Also, speaking of Josh, we went for a walk last night, and he asked me to be his girlfriend."

"Oh! That's great, right?"

"Yeah, I told him I wanted to be his girlfriend eventually but maybe we should go on some dates first," she said with a giggle.

"How did he take that?"

"He was fine. It has been an emotional week. He knows I am there for him. I actually picture us being endgame."

"Really? Well, actually, I do, too. In fact, I didn't realize that you haven't been on dates yet."

"Only that one drive-in date this summer when we were the overflow car for an after-work outing so I don't count that one. He agreed to ask me out on some real dates."

Amie and Hope chatted more and discussed Hope's potential relationship with a boy named Conner. Hope knew that he was interested, but she wasn't ready to have a boyfriend quite yet.

"Yeah," said Amie, "you'll know when you are ready. I assume you are going to the service today?"

"Yes, I have been helping Aunty Nola get some of the stuff ready. She has quite a team working with her. I need to get back to the stadium to help."

"I'll drive you and help for awhile. Then, I'll go home and get dressed. The resort staff is sitting together in the same row since Tanner worked as a busser at Stillwaters."

"Oh, that makes sense," Hope said. "Let's pay and get out of here."

After they paid, Amie drove them to the stadium parking lot where Aunty Nola was in her element, holding a clipboard and organizing the table set up on the freshly-cut lawn and directing volunteers where to put things. Hope and Amie put green and gray plastic table coverings onto the tables and taped them down so that the wind didn't blow them away. Huge crowds were expected to come to the service, so they needed a lot of tables for the buffet lines.

When the covers were in place, Amie said goodbye to Hope and Aunty Nola and went home to get ready, so she could be on time to join her parents, Josh, and the rest of the resort staff.

****

Amie looked at herself in the mirror and was pleased with her look. She had a long, straight cotton skirt, an ivory blouse, and a navy blue pull-over sweater that she draped over her back. She rolled the ends of the sleeves together in front of her and loved the way the ensemble came together. *It's not as somber as a funeral outfit, but it has the proper level of seriousness*, she thought.

"Amie, we've got to go!" her mom called up the stairs.

"Coming!" Amie shouted as she dashed down the stairs, almost slipping near the end, but grabbing the banister to steady herself.

She got into the car with her parents and headed to the stadium. Once they arrived, she joined the other resort staff in a section they had reserved ahead of time with the blessing of Tanner's parents.

Amie saw Josh immediately when she walked in. His light blond hair, so similar to her own, stood out in the crowd. She was still a little miffed because he didn't take her on a date last night, but she tried to let it go and be understanding about his parents' desires to hang out with him on his last night in Chelan before college.

She walked up to him. He looked her over from head to toe, and she blushed.

"You look great, Amie. Wanna sit here?" Josh asked.

"Sure," she agreed and took the seat next to his. Amie was amazed how handsome he looked in his dark slacks and button-down shirt and black tie. *All forgiven,*

Amie thought to herself with a slight smile. Soon, other staff filtered in. Several of the resort staff members had to stay and keep the resort working, but Debbie ensured that everyone who knew Tanner was able to get away. "It is fun to see so many of the staff all in one place. We are usually all spread out in different buildings. It's too bad that it is for such terrible circumstances," Amie commented.

"I was thinking the same thing," Josh confirmed, his sapphire-blue eyes meeting hers. His obvious sadness hurt her heart.

Amie looked around the stadium. There were big screens set up with photos of the boys, senior pictures for the ones who had already had them taken and other pictures for the other boys. The four boys' immediate families were seated in the front rows.

The pastor got up first and welcomed everyone, greeted them, then explained the difference between a celebration of life and a funeral. He said, "If we are Christians, the Bible tells us we grieve, but not like those who have no hope." He shared that God is not willing that any should die, but that all come to repentance, and he hoped that all four of the boys had made that decision.

He then introduced the football coach, who gave a moving speech, where he highlighted stories about each of the boys, which enabled the crowd to know each boy a little better. Some of the stories were humorous, and Amie and Josh laughed aloud with the crowd.

Then Mr. Hawk, the AD, also gave a speech, then a representative from each of the four families spoke. Bryan's parents let his long-time girlfriend Sierra speak on behalf of their family since none of them liked the spotlight. She delivered an eloquent talk of meeting Bryan and what he meant to her. She talked about his relationship with his family and how he loved them. She closed by saying how much both she and Bryan's family would miss him and how sad she was that his hopes and dreams were cut short. "I'll always miss you, Bryan." She closed and blew a kiss to the smiling picture of him on the screen. Amie didn't know Sierra well but she knew that Hope was on the soccer team with her. She admired by the love Sierra had for Bryan.

Tanner's speech was given by his cousin Hollie. She shared that they grew up together because their grandma had a house on the lake, and they played together all the time. As they grew older, they didn't see each other as much, but they texted a lot, and when she went off to WSU last year, he visited a couple times and she gave him a tour. She was looking forward to having him on campus with her next year and was sad that they would have to wait until Heaven to be reunited again. Her talk had some funny moments and some sad moments, and it captured the essence of Tanner perfectly.

After the family representatives spoke, four other preselected friends were called up to give their speeches on behalf of the boys. Ryan Sanders, ASB president, as well as Amie's friend and the boy whom Kendi and Emma had gotten to know this past summer, gave the speech for Tyson. He started by saying that he wished that this speech could be given by Tanner because Tanner and Tyson were like two peas in a pod, and they did everything together. However, it was only fitting that they would end up leaving this world together as well. Amie saw Josh nod when he said that part. Ryan shared stories about times spent together, talked abut the love that Tyson had for his family and friends, and also mentioned how excited Tyson had been to start dating his new girlfriend Kari. He looked at Kari, who was seated in the second row, and said, "Kari, I know he really liked you because he talked about you nonstop for weeks before we convinced him to ask you out. After you started dating, he became much more confident, and you could tell he was especially happy because of you. Thanks for that." He looked up at Tyson's picture on the screen. "Tyson, buddy, having to take your place on the football team sucks. I think you owe an apology to the whole town for that." The crowd laughed. "But seriously, you were the best, and we are gonna miss ya, man. Thanks for being a friend." He set the mic down on the podium. Amie was so proud of Ryan for the tribute he gave for Tyson.

"Which friend is speaking for Tanner?" Amie whispered to Josh.

"Ben is going to do it. His parents asked me if I wanted to speak, and I said I was positive I would fall apart on stage. They understood and said that Hollie was doing the family speech for them for the same reason. I suggested they ask Ben, and they thought that was a good idea. I didn't want to say no, and I feel guilty, but I was so emotional when they asked me."

"Don't worry. Ben will do great," Amie quietly assured him.

Ben stepped up to the podium and, as predicted, gave an outstanding tribute to Tanner, mentioning his love of "family, football, and girls—in no particular order." That line received a chuckle, several nods, and *mmm-hmmm*s from those who knew Tanner well. Ben mentioned some of the fun times they had through the years and told a few stories of pranks they pulled and fun they had that included Josh. Amie was relieved to know that Josh was brought up in the tribute since he and Tanner were such close friends.

There was a song performed by a senior girl while a slide show played with each of the boys' childhood and teenage pictures scrolling by. The photography teacher at the high school had edited a picture of the four boys together in their football uniforms with a background of an angel spreading its wings over them. It was the closing photo in the slide show, and it was an emotional way to close the service. The pastor said a final prayer and dismissed everyone to go to the reception.

Amie and Josh walked out together and stood single file in one of the seven identical buffet lines. The line moved slowly, but that gave them a chance to recap the service. When it was finally their turn, they grabbed plates and filled them up with a delicious array of catered food. Looking around, Amie thought that Aunty Nola's estimate that half of the town would be coming through the lines might be accurate. Josh's mood seemed lighter than it had all week, and it appeared that he had some closure after the service. Amie realized that they would probably need to find seats in the grass and was glad that she had chosen a dark skirt instead of a light-colored one in case she got grass stains on it.

Once they found seats in the grass under an evergreen tree, Josh turned to Amie and said, "We are leaving right after this. My dad's SUV is crammed full of my stuff."

"Wow!" Amie remarked, trying to be excited for him while shielding her own disappointment.

"Are you going to miss me?" he put his fork down.

Amie tried to be lighthearted. "Of course, I will. You're my favorite waiter at Beaches."

The look on Josh's face showed that he wasn't amused by Amie's flippant remark. "No, really, will you miss me?"

Amie realized he wanted a serious answer. "Yes, I will. I'm looking forward to going on some dates with you. Hopefully, that will still happen."

"It will totally happen. I'll be home at least two weekends a month to work, and I hope that they will give me daytime shifts so we can go out together after I get off work. You are my priority." The way he sounded and the look he had in his eyes gave her a shiver between her shoulders and made her feel special.

"That sounds good," Amie smiled. "I know you'll be super busy when you are at school, but I'm always a text away if you want to talk."

Josh had resumed eating his food and nodded when she made that comment. He took a bite from a brownie on his plate and brushed the crumbs off his shirt.

"You can text and call me, too. Let me know how things are going around here."

"I will," Amie promised.

Josh and Amie then saw his parents and older brother walking up to them.

"Hi Amie, how are you?" Josh's mom asked.

"Doing well, thank you, Mrs. Nelson. You look great! How are you?"

"Much better. I never got a chance to thank you for driving up to the hospital and sitting in the waiting room when I was in the ER. Thank you for being there for Joshua," she replied.

"It was my pleasure," Amie assured her.

"Well, it's about time to go, Josh," his dad urged.

"Okay, I'll meet you at the car." His parents and brother went off in the direction of the parking lot, and Josh and Amie got up and dusted off their clothes.

He just looked at her. "Um. I guess you better get going," Amie reminded him.

"Yeah, well, give me a hug." He didn't wait for an answer, and he put his arms around her shoulders and drew her into an embrace. She felt so tiny in his arms.

She hugged him back and faintly smelled his cologne. She breathed it in, enjoying the musky fragrance.

He reluctantly let her go. "Bye, Amie!" he called as he loped to the car to join his family.

"Bye, Josh!" she called. She sat down under the tree and rewound their entire conversation. She wanted it to be etched in her brain so she could replay it over and over whenever she missed him—especially the hug.

CHAPTER FOUR

Fire!

Amie and her family stayed after the Celebration of Life reception to help Aunty Nola clean up the littered plates and cups that were carelessly left around by a small fraction of the attendees.

Afterwards, Amie's dad Randy dropped her and her mom off at home, and he went back to the resort to work on some proposed structural modifications that an architect was drawing up for the resort. Amie's mom Staci had gone into her home office to work on some of her clients' taxes. Amie went upstairs to work on a US History report. She did some online research and was able to crank out the outline for the report and fill in some of the information for the footnotes, so it would be ready when she wrote the paper.

She then shifted gears from history and began studying her Spanish. She found that she had to constantly review her Spanish words, or she would forget them. Spanish didn't come particularly easy for her, but she was determined not to let it ruin her grade point average.

After Spanish, she turned her attention to an English essay that would be due in a week. It was based on a novel that they were supposed to have read over the summer. Amie had looked at the assigned reading earlier in the summer, but she never finished it. She had tried to read a little of it each night since school had started, so she would be able to write her essay. She was almost finished with the book, but didn't have a good direction for the essay.

After a while, she heard the door leading into the kitchen from the garage open and close, then she heard her dad getting a glass of water. She assumed that her mom had already gone to bed.

Her dad called up, "Goodnight, Amie!"

She yelled, "Goodnight, Dad!" She saw that it was already past ten, and she was tired of doing homework. She had been hoping to get a text from Josh, but none had come through yet. She figured he was probably busy getting to know his roommate, and she doubted that she would hear from him until at least tomorrow afternoon.

She decided to read her Bible and write in her journal for a few minutes. She took some time and read in

Ecclesiastes about how there is a time for every purpose under Heaven. She reflected back to the service and wrote down some of her thoughts in her journal. Before she knew it, the clock said eleven, and she turned off her light and went to bed.

****

Sometime after she had gone to sleep, she heard her mom's phone ring. Her mom often left her phone on the charger in the kitchen. Even all the way upstairs in her bedroom, Amie heard her mom pick up the phone, and then she heard her talking in an urgent voice in the kitchen. Amie strained to hear what she was talking about. She heard the words "police," "fire department," "east wing," and "insurance." Amie knew something big was going down. She put on her robe and rushed downstairs. Her mom was fully dressed and looked like she was about to go to the garage.

"What happened?!" Amie cried as soon as it was apparent her mom was off the phone.

"There was a fire at the resort. Everyone has been evacuated. I'm going there now. Dad is there already."

"Can I come?" Amie begged.

"If you can be dressed in two minutes!"

Amie ran upstairs and threw on some jeans and a golf shirt in record time. She grabbed a light jacket and bounded down the stairs, two at a time. She jumped into the passenger seat of the car, where her mom was waiting for her with the garage door open and the car engine running. They sped to the resort and got there in minutes.

Amie's mom parked across the street because there were several emergency vehicles there already, including two fire engines with flashing lights and a couple ambulances. Amie and her mom took in the scene with wide eyes. There were flames shooting from a strip of guest rooms that were separated from the rest of the rooms in the resort by grassy areas. One of the emergency personnel affixed yellow "CAUTION: KEEP OUT" tape to a pole on the side of the parking lot and was rolling it out. When he had successfully blocked off the parking lot, he unrolled a few more feet, cut off the plastic, and tied the end of the tape to a well-placed gutter pipe. Amie and her mom stood behind the tape, frozen in horror.

Amy's eyes darted around the crowd and she craned her neck for signs of Uncle Bob, Aunt Debbie, or her dad. She was rewarded with a glimpse of Jim, one of the maintenance guys who worked for her dad. He was arguing with the fire chief who was pointing to an area that was being cordoned off with yellow tape. The fire chief was urging Jim to get behind the line. Jim reluctantly agreed, but he continued to try to help from behind the tape as he yelled information to whichever emergency personnel happened to be hurrying by at the moment.

A medic was working with a man who was sitting by an ambulance. The man looked elderly, and the medic was giving him some oxygen while an older lady, presumably his wife, hovered next to him, clutching a large suitcase. Amie's eyes were glued to the man and his companion, who remained by his side. Even from a distance, Amie could see the lady's hands trembling as she clutched the luggage. Amie mentally uttered a prayer for the couple as well as all the first responders.

Aunt Debbie emerged from her office with a printout on a clipboard, which she handed to the chief with a pen. Amie assumed that the printout had a list of all the guests who were staying in the wing with their room numbers and registered vehicles. Amie had run that report more than once for various reasons, but definitely not for anything like this. Debbie gave him an animated explanation pointed to things on the printout. Amie was trying to guess by Debbie's movements what she was saying. She guessed that her aunt was informing him of the guests who she knew had already left the premises at the first sound of the smoke alarm. Amie knew that there were several guests in that wing this weekend.

She surveyed the fire. From where she stood, it looked like two suites were fully engulfed in flames, and the adjacent suites were starting to catch fire as well. The fire chief got the information he needed from Debbie and shooed her to safety behind the yellow tape. Amie and her mom ran up to her.

"WHAT HAPPENED?!" Staci cried.

"I don't know for sure, but I think there were a group of guests in room 220 who were partying, and they must have been smoking something. There had been noise complaints about them earlier in the evening, but when Brenda called, they promised to quiet down, and they did. Anyway, the smoke alarms started going off at eleven o'clock. Jim was on duty and hurried over, and he saw that this was a legitimate fire, not just burnt popcorn, and he summoned help and called us and you guys. Randy arrived when we did, and he and Bob immediately started evacuating rooms until the firefighters showed up and took over."

"Where are they?" Staci demanded to know.

"They are on the lake side behind the caution tape." Aunt Debbie replied. Amie looked around, and quite a crowd had gathered with guests from neighboring hotels and people who just heard the sirens or the buzz on their police scanners. "The chief said that they have called up the volunteer fire fighters and crews from Quincy and Wenatchee are coming because they can't afford to let this get out of control," Aunt Debbie added. "It has been such a dry summer that it will consume the town if they don't get it out right away."

"Are all the guests out?" Amie asked.

Aunt Debbie nodded. "Yes, I think so."

They saw the medic release the older gentleman from oxygen and watched him and his wife carefully make their way to the safety behind the caution tape. Debbie rushed over and helped them navigate the caution tape.

"How are you guys?" Debbie asked. "I'm Debbie Larson, the general manager. Let me help you get checked into another room in one of the other hotels."

"We are Sandy and Herb Walker. I think we want to leave town now," the lady replied. "We had gone to bed early, so we've gotten plenty of sleep already. We're worried that the fire will spread, so we want to get back home to Oregon. We were going to be checking out this morning, anyway. We just have to figure out how to get our car released from the parking lot.

"Do you have the keys?" Debbie asked.

"Right here," Herb said, and he reached into his pocket, jangled his keys, and pointed to his sedan. He dropped the keys into Debbie's open hand.

"Let me see what I can do," Debbie promised. She then ducked under the caution tape and approached the chief. "These folks need their car, so they can go back to Oregon. Can I grab it for them?"

The chief frowned, but he nodded, and Debbie hurried toward the sedan before he could change his mind. Staci unhooked the caution tape, and when Debbie drove the car up to the parking lot exit, Staci walked to the other side of the driveway with the tape, allowing the sedan to pass through. She rushed to re-attach the tape, so the scene would remain secure.

Herb and Sandy got into the car that Debbie exited, giving Debbie a quick hug as they did so. "We'll see you next year," they promised as they drove out of town.

The flames had died down at this point, and it looked like the fire department might be winning this battle. Amie saw fire fighters remove a middle-aged man on a stretcher from one of the rooms. He was wearing a pajama pants and no shirt. *He may have passed out from smoke inhalation*, Amie guessed. They put him in an ambulance, and one of the medics got out and removed the caution tape like Staci had done earlier, so the ambulance could drive to the hospital. Amie wondered where his family was.

Speaking of family, she wanted to see what her dad was doing. "Mom, can I go to the back and see Dad?"

"Yes. I'll go with you," Staci replied. The two of them followed the sidewalk and traced the caution tape that went around the perimeter of the resort. Amie was glad to see that the ambulances were not needed, except for the oxygen for Herb and the one gentleman who was taken to the hospital. When they reached the lake side of the resort, they saw that a larger group of people had congregated there than the crowd in front of the resort. Many of the resort's guests, all wearing various sleeping attire, had lined the lake path, holding blankets and random belongings that they had grabbed as they were evacuated. Amie and Staci looked for people who might need blankets or other care.

She was going to run into the laundry room to get some spare blankets, but she realized that she could not breach the caution tape, and it would be ill-advised to try to sneak into a burning building. She tried to remember what they had in their car that could help. She thought she had a Chelan High blanket in the car and asked her mom if she could go get it for some of the guests. Her mom agreed, and Amie dashed to get it.

When she arrived at her mom's car, she opened the trunk and discovered that they had two blankets, both her Chelan High one and a Seahawks one. There were also some Costco non-perishable items that her mom had failed to unpack from her car after her last run into Wenatchee. Amie saw that there was a case of bottled water, a case of granola bars, and some packets of a fruit and vegetable juice blend, so she stacked the boxes together with the blankets, and trudged down the path to the lake with the provisions, barely able to see over the tall stack.

Her dad saw her coming and ran over to help. He grabbed the case of water and two boxes out of Amie's weary arms. She breathed a sigh of relief. "Thanks, Daddy! I thought I was going to trip and fall."

"No problem, Honey. Let's get these passed out to people. But try to focus on hotel guests and not the onlookers since we have limited supplies." Amie agreed, and her mom joined her in passing out the food and drinks to grateful recipients.

After she had passed out all the provisions in her arms, Amie saw a disheveled girl who looked about her age who was sitting on the edge of the path looking devastated. She was wearing a long football jersey t-shirt that she had likely been sleeping in. Amie sat down next to her, wrapped her in the Chelan blanket, and offered her a granola bar and some water. The girl grabbed the water bottle, twisted it open, and gulped it. "Thanks," she mumbled.

"You're welcome," Amie replied. "Which room?"

"Room 220, I think," she said. Amie realized that was the room where the fire originated, but before she could consider that further, the girl continued: "I was hanging out with some guys I met in Quincy who were coming this direction. We drove here, and we were partying a bit. I finally changed into this nightshirt and fell asleep in a chair. I woke up when some men burst through the sliding door, shook me awake, and pulled me out of there. I looked around, and the other guys were all gone. They had just left me there to burn, I guess."

"Are they still around?" Amie demanded.

"No. A police officer came and talked to me and asked for a description of the car. When he radioed it to someone, they said no car like that was in the parking lot. I think the guys I was with started the fire and couldn't put it out, so they ran to the parking lot and drove away! I'm afraid the cops are going to come after me because I was in the room where the fire started."

"Oh my goodness!" Amie exclaimed.

The girl had tears in her eyes. "I smoked with the guys," she confessed. "That's why I didn't wake up when the alarms went off. I had drugs in my system."

"Oh," Amie replied, not sure how to respond. She shot an arrow prayer to God, asking for the right words to say to best help to this girl. She looked at her phone for the time. 5:30. She would normally be getting up for school in a half hour, but she didn't feel tired at all.

"Do you go to school?" Amie asked.

"No. I graduated a year and a half ago from school in Cali. I moved out after I graduated and hitched a ride with a semi, and we ended up in Washington. I've been hanging out with truckers ever since. Most of them were ok—only a few creeps."

Amie attempted a facial expression to create the illusion that she heard stories like this every day.

However, she was fairly certain her expression was a fail when the girl said, "Nevermind. Thanks for the water and this," she pointed to the granola bar.

Amie did not want to lose her connection to the girl, so she said, "My name is Amie. What's yours?"

"Bella," the girl responded, "as in Twilight. It's actually Annabelle, but that sounds like an old porcelain doll, so I changed it to Bella."

"Bella means beautiful," Amie murmured.

"Ya. Probably not a good name for me," she retorted.

"No, you are beautiful! You have great skin and pretty blue eyes. God made you gorgeous."

"God. I haven't heard that name for a while, at least not in that context."

"Well, that's the context I use," Amie replied. "He created you to be a beautiful person, inside and out."

"Oh," Bella huffed.

Amie took a quick look around. She could no longer see flames coming from the building, but the smoke was still pervasive. The east wing of the hotel was charred beyond recognition.

Amie looked at the building sadly and decided to try again with Bella: "Bella, think of this building. Just a few hours ago, this wing was beautiful and now it is demolished. But it will be repaired and will look better than ever. Did you know that God can do that with our lives? The Bible says that God can make beauty from ashes. And you are meant to be beautiful—your name even says it." Bella was staring at her feet on the asphalt of the lake path. Amie knew she was at a pivotal point, and she looked around for her mom, aunt, or another adult who could help her, but she didn't see anyone. She breathed another silent utterance to God: *Help!*

Amie heard a response in her mind, *You have everything you need.*

Amie nodded.

"Bella, I don't know if you know anything about God…" she started.

"Um, yeah, my dad is a pastor; that's why I left town," Bella responded.

Yikes! Now what do I say? Amie decided to be bold, so she said, "Bella, you've heard all this before. That is why I am convinced that you realize that us meeting is more than just chance. God arranged for this all to happen to bring you to a place where He can help restore you to the beauty that He created you to be."

"I don't know…" Bella began.

"Do you trust me?" Amie asked her pointedly.

Bella took a good look at Amie, who was staring at her earnestly. "Yeah, I guess. I don't really know you."

"I know. But I know a lady who can help you. I lived with her this past summer, and she is so helpful to me all the time. Would you be willing to talk with her?"

"I guess so," Bella responded. "I'm stuck here anyway, according to that cop."

"Okay. I'll call her." Amie stepped away and called Aunty Nola, knowing she would be up by now.

"Of course, I'll be right there!" Nola responded. "I smelled smoke, but I had no idea where it was coming from. I was just doing my daily Bible reading."

"Let me guess. Beauty from Ashes in Isaiah?"

"No," Aunty Nola stated. "Fruits of the Spirit in Galatians. This is my New Testament day. Why?"

"Oh, nothing," Amie laughed.

"I'll be right over, Amie."

"Thanks, Aunty Nola," Amie replied. She then hung up and turned back to Bella.

They struck up a conversation about Bella's time on the road, all the states she had visited, and the experiences she had. She had seen almost every state and had visited lots of landmarks, courtesy of one of the truck drivers who treated her like the daughter he never had. He brought her to Yellowstone, Yosemite, the Mall of America, and The Grand Ole Opry during her stint on the road with him. "He was really good to me," she revealed. "He wanted me to go back to my parents, so I told him I would, and he dropped me off where I told him they lived, but I told him the wrong address because I didn't want to go home.

"I wonder where he is now?" Amie asked, thinking he might be at some cool national monument.

"I saw his truck pop up on my newsfeed last week, at least, I'm almost positive that it was his truck. I guess the driver had fallen asleep and crashed into a car not far from here and killed all the passengers. They probably went to your school."

Amie's face lost all its color. Her jaw hurt, and the muscles in her shoulders and arms turned to mush. She remained silent, partially because she couldn't speak, even if she had wanted to.

"That's why I came here. If it was my friend had killed those kids, I figured he was in jail here, so I wanted to talk to him. He was such a nice guy. I'm pretty sure something like this would devastate him."

Amie was officially freaked out. Just then, she saw Aunty Nola walking down the path towards her. She felt relief at seeing her, and relief that the subject could change, if only just a little bit.

"Hi, Amie. It looks like that fire did a lot of damage," Aunty Nola remarked.

Amie gave her a hug, then said, "Yes, it did, but I don't think there were any serious injuries. They did take a gentleman to the hospital. Hopefully, he is okay." Turning towards Bella she said, "Aunty Nola, this is Bella; Bella, this is Aunty Nola. She's not really my aunt, but we calls her that because she loves everyone."

Aunty Nola turned her attention to Bella, and the two began to talk. Amie looked around and saw her mom and Aunt Debbie, and she wandered the short distance to where they were standing.

"Amie, there is nothing more we can do here. Let's go home," her mom suggested.

Amie stole a sidewise glance back to Aunty Nola and Bella. She saw they were getting up and walking towards one of the police officers. Amie asked her mom to wait just a second. She ran over to Aunty Nola.

"My mom wants me to go home with her ..." Amie started.

"No worries. We are going to see if it is okay for me to take Bella home to get a shower and a nap in one of the guest rooms. I'm sure it will be fine. She has been sitting here for hours. We'll be okay."

"Thanks, Amie," Bella said, raising her hand and giving her a fist bump.

Not exactly my style of goodbye, but hey, Bella has been hanging out with truckers, Amie thought passively.

On the way home, and for an hour afterwards, Amie and her mom took turns telling each other all about their morning. She omitted the part about Bella possibly being a former passenger in the truck that killed the students. She didn't know if she was for certain and besides, what good would it do to bring this up at this point. She vowed to keep in touch with Bella and find out more after Bella had a chance to follow up with the semi driver. Amie shared everything about her new friend Bella, and her mom gave her details they learned about the extent of the damage and the repairs that would be needed. She told Amie that she should skip school today, and they both went up to bed.

Amie asked, "What about Dad?"

"He needs to be at the resort for a couple of hours, then he'll come home and sleep for awhile, too."

"Mmmm, good," Amie murmured sleepily, then made her way up the stairs that seemed endless. Once she made it up, she crawled into bed and slept for the next six hours.

****

When Amie woke up, she looked at her phone and saw that she had 22 missed texts and 14 missed calls, and she had slept through all of them.

She listened to her voicemails. Everyone at school had heard about the fire, and, when Amie didn't show up at school and didn't answer her texts, a rumor got started that she was in the hospital because she had been trapped in the building during the fire. Amie laughed at how ridiculous the story had become and then set about doing damage control. She ended up writing one long text and copying and pasting it to all the people who had tried to communicate with her over the last few hours.

Then, she went downstairs to talk to her parents. Her mom was awake and working in her office.

She updated Amie about the status of the resort: "Dad came home a couple hours ago, and he is sleeping now. The fire investigators determined that the fire was started in room 220 due to drug use. The restoration company is already hard at work fixing up the east wing. The other areas of the resort did not sustain damage, just a lot of soot. The restaurant staff members are cleaning Beaches and Stillwaters. They will remain closed today, but they will reopen again tomorrow. The rest of the resort is getting a thorough cleaning to remove soot, and guests can return to their rooms if they want to once their room has been cleaned."

"How is Dad doing?"

"He is doing fine, but he was exhausted, so hopefully, he can catch up on his sleep. He will be needed at the resort big time in the coming days.

"What about Bob and Debbie?"

"They are exhausted, too, but they are trying to hold everything together. Debbie wondered if you would mind filling in at the front desk today."

"Not at all!" Amie exclaimed. "Can I take your car?"

"Yes, but we need to get you your own pretty soon," Staci remarked.

"Works for me!" Amie agreed on her way out to the garage.

****

When she got to the resort, Debbie briefed her on what she wanted her to do.

"Thank goodness you're here, Amie," Debbie said. "I hope you got some good rest. I'm going to have you take over for me, so I can pick George up from middle school so I can help him sort out the truth about what happened from the rumors that are probably circulating around his middle school. I'm thinking we could probably use some mother-son time! I also need to sleep for a while. Basically, I just want you to take incoming calls and help them as best you can. Make sure you look up their reservation first and see what is written in the notes before you talk to them. I have a script that you can use to help you when you talk with people. It has the questions that most people are asking. Just look up their reservation and see where they were scheduled to stay and move them to another room, if necessary, and let them know you have them taken care of. If their reservation is for January or later, tell them they will be in the same room, but it will be freshly renovated, so it will be like a brand-new hotel room."

"Perfect! I can do that," Amie assured her.

"I have Brenda and Linda both here, and they'll be reaching out to guests who are coming in the next two weeks to tell them what is going on, and they'll also be helping walk-in guests. Brenda will stay for the night shift, and you and Linda can leave after Brenda gets a dinner break."

"Okay! We'll be fine. Go rest, Debbie!"

"See ya later – you're the best!" Debbie assured them as she walked out the door toward the parking lot to go home to see her son George and get some much-needed rest.

Amie spent the afternoon fielding calls from current and upcoming guests regarding the fire and found the script Debbie left to be really helpful.

Things had slowed down by six o'clock, and Linda and Amie stuck around, so Brenda could get some dinner. When she returned, they went back home with assurances from Brenda that she could handle things.

Amie stopped by The Guesthouse to see how Bella was doing, but no one was home. Amie shrugged and figured they were out to dinner. *Mmmm, dinner sounds good. I'd better head home.*

****

When Amie arrived home, she walked into the kitchen, lured by the tantalizing smell of pizza baking in the oven. Her dad and mom were sitting at the table discussing the events of the day.

"Hi, Dad! How's everything going?"

"Pretty good, despite the obvious," he grinned ruefully. "It could have been a lot worse. The guy who had to go to the hospital was released, and he is fine. The wing is getting rebuilt. It had needed a facelift anyway, so this just dictated the timing. I'll probably be working long hours at the resort for the next few months, but that will help to make up for being an absentee manager this past summer when I was in Montana with Grandpa Peterson. How did your shift go, Amie?" he asked.

"Good! I think all the guests were supportive, and they were just curious about what was going on. People were calling from everywhere. It is crazy how fast news spreads. Speaking of that, did you hear the rumor that went around school that I was trapped in the fire?"

"I actually got some calls about that from moms," Staci replied with a laugh. "I was happy to assure them that you were fine. Praise God, *everyone* is fine."

Randy's phone. It was his brother Bob, who asked if they could come over and chat about the resort.

Randy responded, "Of course! We'll throw another pizza in the oven. Bring George with you!"

The timer rang, and Amie leaped up and grabbed some fall-colored potholders from the drawer and pulled the bubbling pizza from off the rack. She found the cutter and sliced the pizza into eight triangles. She pulled another pizza from the freezer, sprinkled some extra cheese on it, and put in the oven, so it would be ready when her relatives arrived. Her cousin George was in the midst of a growth spurt and he could eat a whole pizza by himself. She brought the first pizza over to the table. She got six plates out and put them on the table so they would be ready when their guests arrived.

"Wow! Thanks, Amie! It is good to have a teenager to wait on me," her mom laughed.

"Thanks," Amie replied. "Now, about that car…"

CHAPTER FIVE

Mall Fun

October arrived and, with it, colder nights. Apple harvest was in full swing, iced teas had been replaced with hot pumpkin spice lattes, and the high school was abuzz with homecoming proposals.

Amie had made it a point to attend every football game so far. She even helped organize a couple rooter buses to travel to the first game since the accident. The game was in Granger, and, when she exited the rooter bus, the first person she saw was her friend from last summer at The Guesthouse, Emma. When the two girls saw each other, they squealed and gave each other big hugs, then sat together on the bleachers to watch the team play. Afterwards, they took a selfie together. Amie also took pictures of the team playing so she could post it for people to see who weren't able to attend the game themselves. That game was a victory, but the next one was a hard loss to a good team.

Josh had arranged to work at Beaches every other weekend. That way, he could come home, make money, and see friends, but still have a somewhat normal college experience.

Amie and Josh were finally able to have their first date, which was to Wenatchee for dinner and a movie, and then a second to a restaurant in nearby Manson. On both dates Josh had held her hand and opened the car doors for her, and on the second date, they had their first kiss in the car in front of her house. It was as exciting as she hoped it would be and Amie was all in. Josh appeared to be equally into her. She did the math and realized that he would be in town for homecoming weekend. She wondered how he would feel about going to a high school homecoming dance, even though he was in college.

She asked him one night when they were talking on the phone: "So, Josh, I was wondering how you felt about attending homecoming this year?"

"The game?" he asked cagily.

"No, not the game—the dance!"

"Well, it would depend on my date …"

"What if it was me?" Amie questioned.

"If that's the case, I would love to go to the dance," Josh confirmed.

"Good, then it's all settled. I can go shopping for my dress! Any color preferences?"

"Uh, no. I'll leave all fashion decisions in your capable hands."

"Okay, I'll keep you posted."

"I'm sure you will," he teased.

They chatted a bit more, then hung up, so they could both catch up on homework. Josh had told her that college so far was quite a bit harder than high school, but it was still manageable. Amie wasn't looking forward to harder classes because she was enjoying the level of classes she had now.

****

Josh was staying at his dorm this weekend, so Amie wanted to make plans with some of her girlfriends. She arranged with Hailey, Lexi, and Amanda to go to Wenatchee for shopping and dinner. Even though the girls had their driver's licenses, Amie's mom said she would drive because she had to meet with a client in Wenatchee and could drop them off at the mall.

On the way to the mall, Amie sat up front with her mom, but spent most of the time with her head facing the back seats, chatting with the other girls. They covered the topics of classes, clothes, boys, and homecoming. They all wanted to find their perfect homecoming dress here because the shopping in Chelan was limited. Stacie reminded the girls not to get a dress that showed too much skin. "Remember to find dresses that are beautiful *and* modest. You don't want us to have to turn around and come back here tomorrow to return a dress that is not mom-approved."

The girls laughed because they wouldn't mind a second trip to the mall, but they recognized her point. "Don't worry mom, we'll get appropriate dresses," Amie assured her.

Staci dropped the teens off in front of Macy's and said she would be back for them in about three hours. She admonished them to stick together and to go ahead and get dinner without her because she would be eating dinner with her clients.

The four girls made a beeline for the formal dress section. They were a little late in the season, and the selection was more limited, but they each found a few that they liked enough to try on. Each of them went to the fitting rooms to try on their dresses, and they agreed to step out and show the others.

Amie went first. The first dress she picked was a form-fitting, long, black mermaid style gown. It was a pretty dress, but the proportions were wrong for Amie's little body, and it would require a lot of altering. She passed it to Lexi to try on. When Lexi emerged from the fitting room, she took everyone's breath away.

"Say yes to the dress!" Amie squealed, and the other girls agreed.

Lexi looked at the price tag and exclaimed, "Yes to the dress, but no to the price!"

In response, Amie opened her cute bronze Michael Kors bag and pulled out some coupons. "25% off for each of us. That might make the price more palatable."

Lexi mentally did the math. "That helps, but it is still a lot of money. I'll have to think about it!"

"If you buy it now, maybe we could do a dress trade for the next dance, so you wouldn't have to buy one that time. Then, you could justify today's purchase." Hailey had several beautiful formal dresses because she seemed to attend almost every dance, so Lexi took her up on that offer.

"How about you, Amanda? Do you like any of your dresses?" Lexi asked.

Amanda peeked her head out. "One is a definite no. One might work, and one is the best of the three, but I'm not sure."

"Show us the best one!" Hailey coaxed.

"Okay, here goes," Amanda agreed and emerged from the room wearing a burgundy tea-length dress with a handkerchief hem and a lace overlay.

"It's stunning!" Lexi crowed.

"Perfection," Amie agreed.

"Definitely get that one," Hailey encouraged.

Amanda blushed from all the attention. This was her first formal dress and the first dance she was going to with a boy. "Okay, you convinced me. But I'll definitely need that coupon!" she laughed.

"You're next, Hailey," Lexi announced. "Choose wisely because I might be borrowing it for prom."

"Oh, well, I've never worn blue, so I'm hoping this light blue one will look good. Otherwise, this blush one might work."

"Hmmm… I'm on team blush for now, but I'll reserve official judgment 'til I can see it on you," Lexi commented.

"Me, too," Amie agreed.

After a brief moment, Hailey emerged with the light blue dress on. "Oooo, that *is* pretty," Lexi gushed.

"I like it, too" Amanda drawled, her childhood spent in Georgia evident.

"Let's see the blush one," Amie encouraged.

They heard a rustling as Hailey took off the blue dress, hung it up, and carefully stepped into the blush one and zipped the back. The creaky fitting room door opened, and the judging panel reviewed the dress and considered whether it was better than the blue one.

"I vote for the blue one," Amanda commented.

"Me, too," Amie agreed.

"I think I like the blush better," Lexi decided.

"I do, too. I think I'll get this one." Hailey went back in the room to put it on the hanger. "Wait, I forgot; I have one other dress in here. I'll try it out for you to see." A moment later, the door opened, and Hailey was wearing a lovely lilac gown that seemed to brighten up her features.

"I changed my mind. This one's my favorite," Amie reconsidered.

"Me, too!" Lexi and Amanda both replied in unison.

"Okay, I like it best as well, so lilac it is! Now, Amie, you are the only one left to decide."

"Here goes!" Amie cried, ducking into the fitting room. She came out a few minutes later in a strappy, short fuchsia dress and announced, "No need to vote— I'm getting this one!" The girls agreed it was a bold choice because it was shorter than a lot of the formal dresses but it was still tasteful on Amie because of her petite stature, and she was pretty sure her mom would approve. The color was equally bold. There were no other dresses in the department with such a striking jewel tone and it was absolutely stunning. "The best part is, it's on clearance and I can still use the coupon, so it is an astounding deal!"

"Nice work, smalls!" Lexie remarked.

"Let's pay and eat!" Amanda suggested.

Amie led the way. When they checked out, they realized that there was an automatic 10% off formal dresses that weren't on clearance, so Amanda, Lexi, and Hailey were able to save a little money and were extra happy as they headed to the food court for dinner.

As they walked down the mall corridors, they could smell the fragrances of cinnamon rolls combined with pizza, Chinese food, French fries, and more. They approached the food court to decide what to get. This area had been newly renovated and it had gray wood floors and gray tables and chairs with ocean-blue accents piping around the table edges. Each restaurant kept their signature looks but the façade under each counter matched the gray and ocean-blue look of the rest of the food court. Amie admired the choices that the designer had made when creating this space. Amanda wanted Pad Thai, Hailey lined up for pizza, Lexi selected a burger, and Amie opted for Chinese food. They each ordered and met back at a square white laminate table in the center court.

"This was a good week to have an away football game, so we could shop," Hailey remarked.

"I'm sure they considered that when they were determining their schedules," Lexi commented.

"No need to get sassy, just sayin'," Hailey retorted.

Amie quickly changed the subject: "Speaking of football, I can't believe how well they are doing. They might actually go to state this year, after all!"

"Wouldn't that be great!" Amanda gushed.

"I know! It is fun to see how well the new players have figured it out and have bonded with the team. Ryan is so hot! I can't believe he is single," Lexi stated.

"I know! Ben, too!" Amanda agreed with her charming accent. "I heard that they weren't even going to Homecoming. Isn't that crazy. Every girl wants to go with them. Except girls with *college* boyfriends."

Amie rolled her eyes playfully in response.

"Our whole football team is pretty attractive," Hailey remarked with her charming accent.

The girls had to agree.

The dinner conversation then turned to their homecoming dates. Hailey was seeing a guy in the junior class named Cameron. They had been dating since last spring. His family had a ranch fifteen minutes out of town, and he was a traditional cowboy who competed at rodeos. He had been homeschooled prior to high school and was a pleasant surprise to the Chelan girls when he showed up for class on the first day of their freshman year. Since then, he hadn't dated anyone until he was assigned to the same computer coding elective with Hailey during second semester of their sophomore year. She learned the class material quickly, but he struggled with it a little bit. Since she sat next to him, she helped him get up to speed, and they got to be friends. She asked him to the Sadie Hawkins dance last March, and they had been casually dating ever since.

"So are things still going well for you two?" Amanda questioned.

"Yeah, I guess so. He is out of town a lot doing rodeos and stuff, but we get together about twice a month. We don't ever see each other at school, so those dates are about it. But every time I think we should just break up, I see him and change my mind." They all laughed at the exasperated face she made.

"So, Amanda, are you excited to go to homecoming with Gabe?" Amie asked.

"Not real-ly," she drawled slowly, which usually indicated hesitation or possible disdain. "I'm excited to *go* to the dance, but I feel awkward goin' with Gabe. I felt like I had to go with him because he asked me in front of people in class, and I didn't want to say no. Plus, like I said, I wanted to go to the dance. I just feel awkward because we've literally never talked to each other ever, and I'm hoping he just wants to be friends."

Amie winced in sympathy. "Oh, that's too bad. Well, hopefully, you will at least become friends through the experience. It's interesting that he asked you when you had never said a word to each other before."

"I know. He probably thought I would be the most likely girl to say yes because I'm...well I'm not..." she trailed off.

"He probably chose you because you are beautiful, smart, and kind," Amie insisted.

"Maybe so," Amanda acquiesced, "but I don't think he is my Prince Charming."

"Speaking of Prince Charming, *Amie*," Hailey segued.

The flush that came to Amie's face was evident against her light hair. "Yeah, Josh is pretty cool," she admitted. "I am looking forward to the dance."

"You two are an adorable couple," Amanda gushed. "You look just alike. If y'all get married and have kids, we know exactly what they'll look like."

"We'll see, we just barely became official so no rush!" Amie laughed, having heard that line a few times already. "Who wants a cinnamon roll?" she asked.

"I'd split one," Lexi replied.

"So would I," Hailey agreed.

"Mmm, me too!" Amanda chimed in.

"Okay, so I'll order two cinnamon rolls and get plastic knives and four forks," Amie decided.

Hailey started to open her purse to get her money out, and Amie brushed her off. "This is my treat, ladies!" she said, then scampered off to get them before any of the girls could argue.

The girls enjoyed their cinnamon rolls and secretly wished they would have ordered a whole one instead of just having a half each.

Lexi looked at her phone. "It's been about two hours. We better get moving if we want to do more shopping."

The girls got up, threw their trash away, and put the red plastic trays in their place on top of the trash bins. The girls split into pairs; Hailey and Lexi went to smell the new fragrances in the lotion store, and Amanda and Amie checked out the makeup counters in a department store. There was a promotion going on at one of the counters, where customers could spend $35 on any of their products and be able to purchase a sparkly bag with sample-sized goodies for $15. Both Amanda and Amie couldn't pass up that deal. Amanda bought some foundation, and Amie bought some pink lipstick.

"We better tell the other girls about this deal before we leave the mall, or they are going to be mad if they miss out!" Amanda pointed out.

"Definitely. Rule number one: always tell your homies about the best shopping deals!" Amie stated, and they both giggled as Amie texted them about the deal.

They walked across the white tiled walkway to the shoe department and tried on stylish black boots to go with their winter wardrobes. Amanda complained because she needed boots that offered the wide calf option, and only a few brands had that. Amie had the opposite problem because she wore a size five shoe, and that size was often hard to find for her. Neither one of them had luck in the boot department, although they ended up going to three stores.

At the end of their designated three hours, everyone ended up at Macy's right on time to meet Amie's mom for the ride home. The ride home consisted of happy chatter and descriptions of all the dresses that they tried on and why they chose the particular dresses that they selected. Amie's mom told her later that night that she really enjoyed hearing about the dress shopping and she was glad that she had occasion to drive into town.

"Thanks, mom! My friends all like you. You are a cool mom!" Amie remarked, and meant it.

CHAPTER SIX

Homecoming Helper

On Saturday, Amie awoke to the sun rising over the lake. She pulled out her Bible, read a few chapters in the book of Luke, and wrote in her journal. She spent some time praying for all of her friends from school and her friends from last summer.

She finished praying and was in the bathroom brushing her teeth when her phone rang. She saw it was Hope. She spit out her toothpaste and picked up the phone on the second ring. "Hi, Hope!" she squealed.

"Hi, Amie!" Amie could hear the grin in Hope's voice and was excited to talk. "I have a slight problem that I thought you might be able to help with," she started.

"Sure, anything!" Amie effused.

"So Conner invited me to homecoming, I realized I don't have a dress, and I also don't have a lot of cash," Hope admitted.

"Okay, I might be able to help. I know a girl named Julie, who was a senior last year, and she is about your height. She probably has a closet full of formal dresses just sitting there. I can see if you could borrow one."

"Are you sure you don't mind asking?" Hope inquired.

"Nope, I'll check right now. Hopefully, she is up!" Amie mentioned, looking at the time on her phone. "Stay tuned, okay?"

Amie decided to text her because it was pretty early on a Saturday morning for a college student. Luckily, Julie was up and was more than generous. She told Amie to let her friend raid her closet and borrow any dress except the navy blue one because she was going to be using that one for a sorority formal. She said she would call her mom and let her know they would be coming and text Amie back to let her know when she would be home. Amie got in the shower and proceeded to get ready for the day.

Pretty soon, she received a text from Julie saying her mom asked if Amie could bring her friend in about an hour. Amie called Hope and told her she would pick her up in an hour to go shopping in Julie's closet.

"Could you pick me up at the sporting goods store?" Hope asked.

"Of course! See ya in an hour!"

An hour later, Amie pulled up to the parking lot of the store, and Hope hopped into the passenger side. The girls chatted enthusiastically about the dance and the way Conner had invited her by planting little footprints made out of yellow construction paper onto the path where Hope would be jogging. Each foot had a separate word in: "Hope, will you go to homecoming with me?" He spaced the little yellow feet apart so Hope would find them as she jogged along the path.

"That was pretty clever, I'll give him credit," Amie admitted.

"What about you?" Hope asked. "I'm assuming you are going with Josh. Oh, wait, isn't he at UW now?"

"Yeah, he is at college, but he is coming back for the homecoming dance. He only has one early class on Fridays, so that makes it easy for him to come back on weekends."

"How're you guys doing with the long-distance thing?"

"So far, so good. We're both busy with homework and stuff, but we talk occasionally. He's not crazy about the Seattle traffic. He's definitely a small-town boy at heart," Amie confided. Then, she remembered what she had been wanting to ask Hope about: "Hope, I saw you in *People Magazine*! I can't believe I didn't know about the money you had found!"

"I know. I wasn't allowed to talk about it until after it came out in the magazine, and then, after it was out, everyone knew, so I just kinda laid low about it."

"Well, are you okay to talk about it now?" Amie demanded.

"Yes," Hope agreed. "What do you want to know?"

"Did the bag of money you discovered when you are out jogging belong to the famous hijacker, or did they prove the connection yet?"

"Yes. I think they proved that it was definitely the hijacker's money, but they aren't sure who he was yet."

"How'd the money get to Chelan?" Amie questioned.

"They think the hijacker might have settled in this area, and it was possible that he just lived in the woods for part of the time and hid the bag there before emerging and starting a new life."

"Wow, that's bizarre! Maybe the guy still lives here?" Amie speculated.

"Who knows?" Hope wondered aloud.

They chatted a little more, and soon, they arrived at Julie's house. Julie's mom was super accommodating.

"Julie had a boyfriend from another school all during high school, so they went to every formal dance at both of the schools," Julie's mom explained. "We didn't think of the trick of borrowing dresses from girls from other schools until her senior year; hence, the closet full of formal dresses. I could open up a store with all these gowns!" The girls laughed at her exasperation that they knew was partially in jest.

They selected a long lime green sleeveless dress from the many that filled the guest closet. Hope tried it on, and it was a perfect fit. Julie's mom said to go ahead and take it and return it the week after the dance. Hope thanked Julie's mom profusely as they left.

On the way back to The Guesthouse, Hope asked Amie what else she needed to take care of for the dance.

Amie explained all the details, including the boutonnière purchase, matching the dress color to the tux accessories, and deciding who is buying the pictures. "Maybe you guys could go to dinner with Josh and me if you want."

"I would love that. I'll mention it to Conner."

Amie brought her home and Hope exclaimed, "Wow, there's a lot of work to go to one dance! Thanks for helping me get this dress, and thanks for the 411 on everything, Amie!"

Amie gave Hope a hug, then drove back to her own house.

****

On Sunday, Amie was at home after church when she got a call from Hope. Hope explained that Kendi's mom and dad won some contests for creating a logo and jingle for the sporting goods store that her uncle was purchasing. Hope went on to explain that Kendi, Mr. and Mrs. Arnold, Emma, and Mr. And Mrs. Martinez would be in Chelan next weekend for the ribbon-cutting ceremony for the new store.

"Eek! The Guesthouse Girls all together again? That's fantastic!" Amie squealed.

"I know, right?" Hope agreed.

Shortly after she and Hope finished their conversation, the phone rang again. She looked down at her screen and saw that it was Kendi.

"Hi, Kendi!" Amie practically screamed into the phone.

"Hey, Amie! Is this a good time to talk?"

"YES!" Amie squealed. "I just talked to Hope, and she said both you and Emma are coming to town this weekend! I can't believe it!"

"I'm excited, too!" Kendi replied. "However, I've got a slight problem." She explained that Ryan had come to Redmond yesterday and found out that it was her homecoming, so he asked if he could take her. Then, she told Amie that Ben found out she was coming to town next weekend for the ribbon-cutting ceremony, and he invited her to Chelan's Homecoming.

"Okay, I'm tracking. What is the problem? Do you think Ryan will be mad that you're going with Ben?"

"Not that as much as I'm worried that Emma will be upset because I'm going with Ben. Hope, you, and I are all going to Chelan's Homecoming, and she will be stuck at The Guesthouse with all of the adults. I don't know what to do."

"Oh, I totally get it." She thought for a moment. "Okay, I think I can fix this. Don't worry. Give me a few minutes, and I'll see if I can work something out. I'll call you back."

Amie called Cody and asked him if he was going to homecoming. He said he was taking a girl named Lily.

"Why? Were you going to ask me?" he inquired.

"No. I'm going with Josh. But I was wondering because I'm going to have a friend in town…oh, never mind. Thanks anyway!"

"Maybe ask Ryan? He doesn't have a date."

"Oh, great idea! Thanks, Cody!" Amie replied. "Bye!" she blurted and hung up.

She called Ryan and told him that all the girls from The Guesthouse would be in town next weekend, and they all had dates for Chelan's homecoming dance except Emma.

"Would you be willing to ask her to the dance?" Amie asked after explaining things.

Ryan was confused. "Okay, I guess, but who is Kendi going with?"

Amie didn't have time to waste. "Ben," she replied.

"Oh, I see how he is. Hmm…okay, I'll call Emma."

"Okay, could you do it now?" Amie asked.

"Yes, I'll do it right now," he assured her.

"I'm sorry, but could you text me when you have done it? Sorry to be a control freak."

"Okay, you do sound a little like that, but yes, I'll call her now, and I'll text you if she says yes."

About ten minutes later, Amie got a text with a checkmark emoji from Ryan. She got another text from him that said, "It's all set for Saturday." Amie assumed that he sent the second text just in case she didn't understand what he meant by the checkmark. She had to giggle. Ryan was so goofy.

Amie then texted Kendi: "Okay. Everything is settled. Ryan didn't have a date (shocking!), so he called Emma, and he is taking her to homecoming! I had asked Cody first, but he is taking someone else. Ryan seemed disappointed that you were going with Ben, but he was happy to take Emma." Amie's fingers flew over the keypad before finally hitting "send."

"Wonderful – Thank u!" came Kendi's quick reply.

Amie was exhausted after helping arrange everyone's homecoming stuff. Then, she thought of homecoming dinner. She hadn't arranged anything for herself and Josh. Since the other three girls just got their dates this weekend, she was sure that none of them had, either. She texted Jonathan, the manager at Stillwaters, and asked if they could possibly find a spot for a table of eight for her and her friends on Saturday night.

He texted back, "Ha ha!"

She thought she'd better go talk to him in person. She dashed downstairs and asked her mom if she could borrow the car to go to the resort. Her mom was buried deep in a spreadsheet and just nodded without asking questions. Amie grabbed the keys from the hook and opened the garage door, hitting the opener so it would be open and ready as she made her retreat out the door.

She drove a little over the speed limit the few minutes it took to get to the resort and darted up the stairs to Stillwaters to talk to Jonathan. The forty-something year old manager was just finishing up the brunch crowd. She put on an adorable facial expression and walked up to him. "Hi, Jonathan," she used her sweetest voice. Jonathan had worked for the resort for about twelve years and was practically a family member.

"Hi, Amie," he said in an even tone that revealed that he knew what she was up to, and he was not going to fall for her tricks.

Amie was pretty sure she would be able to talk him into it, though. "So, Jonathan, I have this problem."

"Oh, I'm sure you do, girl!" he played along.

"You see, I really need to get a table for homecoming for me and my friends."

"Uh huh, and how is this my problem?" he teased.

"Um, did I mention the table would include one of your best waiters, Josh, who comes home from college every other weekend to work shifts here?"

"Okay, now you have my attention," Jonathan responded.

"So, is there a way that we could squeeze one more table for eight into your crowded reservation book for next weekend? We wouldn't be picky about the time, and we could eat quickly and even bus our own table, so you could turn it quicker."

"Okay, Miss Amie." He consulted the booking list. "You guys can come in at six o'clock. I might call you with another time if we have some movement in the schedule this week. Will that work?"

"YES!" she squealed, giving him a big hug.

"Okay, okay," Jonathan extracted himself from her hug. "But you will NOT bus your own table – got that?"

"Okay! Thank you so much Jonathan! We'll see ya then!"

Amie drove home at a leisurely pace, then went up to her bed to resume work on her history report that she kept trying to finish. However, instead of finishing it, she started to fall asleep, so she decided to take a nap and stay up late tonight to finish the report.

She texted Hope, Kendi, and Emma that she took the liberty of arranging dinner for the eight of them at Stillwaters, but if any of them wanted to do their own thing, they just needed to let her know. She got texts back from each of them in quick succession, thanking her for the arrangements.

Wow, arranging homecoming for four different couples is a tiring proposition! Amie thought before closing her eyes to rest.

CHAPTER SEVEN

Homecoming Weekend

Amie had a hard time concentrating at school with all the excitement of homecoming, and Friday was especially crazy. Luckily, they had a pep assembly on Friday and announced the homecoming court. Amie hadn't been nominated this year and had not won the title in the previous two years either so she hoped she might be on the slate for her senior year. However, she was excited to see that Cody would be crowned the Homecoming King, and her friend Hannah was the Junior Princess.

Josh was coming home for the weekend. Amie planned to stop by the resort on her way home from school because he would already be there working his shift. She was itching to see him. She was excited because after she met up with Josh, she and Hope would be reunited with Kendi and Emma, and the four of them were going to the game together. Never in her dreams could she have predicted such a scenario.

After school, she rushed to the resort and saw Josh. He was rolling silverware into napkins to prepare for the dinner rush. He looked even more handsome that the last time she saw him, if that was even possible.

Jonathan saw her come in and Amie heard him say, "Go ahead and take your fifteen-minute break, Josh. I think Amie might want to see you!"

Amie ran up to Josh and gave him a hug, and then the two of them walked outside for a quick chat.

"I am so glad to see you! Did you have a good drive home? I'm so excited for the dance. The other Guesthouse Girls will be here in a couple hours, and we are going to the game!"

"Geez, Amie! You are making me tired just listening to you," he playfully complained with a grin.

"Okay," she slowed *way* down. "How are you?"

"It was fine," he replied. "Are you excited?" he joked.

That set Amie off again, and she talked a mile a minute about the arrangements for the game tonight and what the plans were for tomorrow, and Josh just looked at her and laughed.

"Okay, girl, you are seriously making me tired. Just tell me when and where, and I will be there. I don't need any more details than that."

"Okay! Call me tonight after you get off work."

"Sounds good, I'll talk to you then." He leaned over and gave her another hug, then went back upstairs to work.

Amie was on cloud nine after seeing Josh, and she went home to get things in order for tonight. She gathered supplies to cheer on the team and put on the outfit she wanted to wear and made sure that her green and gray nails still looked good. They just had to last until tomorrow morning when she would apply her new fuchsia polish that perfectly matched her formal dress. She chatted with her mom for a bit and made sure they were planning on going to the ribbon-cutting ceremony tomorrow.

"Of course, we are definitely coming to the ribbon cutting. Business owners always support other business owners on these types of things," Staci replied. "It will be fun to see what he does with the place. I'm sure it will have more of a marine feel since he will tie it into the boat rental business."

"Yes, he is renaming it 'Everything Outdoors.'"

"Oh, yeah, I remember that from the logo contest, not that I have any talent in that area."

"Maybe not, but he might need you to do his taxes."

"Yikes, I hope not but I have had a meeting with him.

The resort's taxes are enough, plus I have three other big clients. Do ya want to be my assistant?" she teased.

"No, mom, I can assure you, I will never be good at accounting. I'm more of a front-of-house-type person."

"That you are, my sweet girl," Staci agreed.

Pretty soon, Amie heard her dad's truck pull into the garage, and her dad came lumbering in. "The guys made a mistake on the paint color today, and I had to go through each unit in the east wing to show them which walls needed to be repainted," he explained.

"Wow, they rebuilt that wing so fast!" Amie remarked.

"They had to," Randy replied. "The cold weather is coming soon, and if they didn't work fast this fall, they would've had to be working in the snow."

"True," Amie replied. "Ready to go?" she asked impatiently.

"Go where?" he teased.

"Dad!" She flounced out of the room, then found her mom. "Mom, can you tell dad we're ready to go?"

"We're ready to go, Randy," Staci laughed.

"Okay, let me clean up." He looked at Amie's impatient face. "Five minutes, I promise!"

In less than five minutes, the Larson family was in Staci's car, driving to The Guesthouse, where the other families had just arrived. The other families didn't know that Aunty Nola had invited the Larsons for dinner, so it would be a little surprise for the girls.

When they pulled up, they knocked on the door, then Amie and her parents burst in. "Room for three more?" Amie's mom asked with a laugh, looking at everyone and all the pizza.

"Of course," Aunty Nola smiled welcomingly.

The girls squealed with excitement when Amie walked in, and they quickly crowded together for the picture Emma's dad took with her phone. Amie and her parents grabbed some pizza and ate it quickly so as not to slow everyone else down.

"It looks like it's about time to head to the game," Amie's dad announced after they'd all chatted awhile.

"Are you ready for some football?" he sang jovially, and everyone laughed.

****

Amie taught the girls the fight song on the way to the game.

"Hopefully, we will need to sing it a lot tonight," Aunty Nola commented. "Ben has been doing such a great job at quarterback, and the other guys have really been doing well, too."

When the group arrived at the game, Staci and Randy told the other adults to follow them to better seats, away from where the students typically sat. "I guarantee that you don't want to sit in that section," she said, indicating the area where Amie and Hope were leading the other girls.

The game got off to a good start. Ben was playing quarterback, and Ryan and Cody were switching out at running back .

The student section was crazier than usual with small town school pride, and Amie and other students had brought banners to hold up, as well as confetti to throw, streamers, glitter, and face paint in the school colors of green and gray.

By half time, the girls had spread green and gray face paint all over their faces as they watched the homecoming court get crowned. Amie and her friends cheered loudly for Hannah when she was crowned the Junior Princess and for Cody when he was named Homecoming King.

The Guesthouse Girls had a blast at the game. They enjoyed socializing with the students sitting near them. Amie caught up with some of her friends that she hadn't seen for a long time. By the end of the game,

Chelan emerged victorious, and the students celebrated. She was glad to see that the other Guesthouse Girls seemed to be having a great time.

When they went back to The Guesthouse after the game, the girls begged Amie to stay with them. Amie's parents suggested she come home with them and reminded her that she could come back first thing in the morning. Amie agreed that she would come back tomorrow morning after she finished her beauty rest. She gave them lots of hugs before she left.

****

The next morning, Kendi and Emma texted Amie that they were headed to Brandon's Coffee and Bakeshop for coffee and that she should come join them. Amie had slept in a bit because she was on the phone until late with Josh. She rolled out of bed and took a quick shower when she saw their text, but it took her a while to get ready for the ribbon-cutting ceremony.

Finally, she was ready and realized she probably missed the coffee date, but she could meet up with them at The Guesthouse. She asked her mom if she could take the car. Her mom agreed.

Amie replied to Emma and Kendi: "Sorry, slept in. I'm on my way now. I'll meet you at The Guesthouse."

Emma and Kendi arrived at The Guesthouse just as Amie was pulling into the driveway.

"Hey, ladies!" Amie said cheerfully. "We have some time before the ribbon-cutting ceremony. Do you want to head to the lake for a little while?"

"Yes!" the girls agreed. "We'll just tell our parents."

Kendi and Emma poked their heads in the front door and secured permission.

The girls decided to walk to the lake because it was a fairly nice day.

"Amie, where was Josh last night?" Kendi asked.

Amie thought back to yesterday afternoon when she spent Josh's fifteen-minute break with him. *Mmmm...he is so adorable*, she thought to herself. She broke out of her little daydream to answer Kendi's question. "He comes back from school sometimes on weekends and works at the resort, and he worked last night, so he'd be able to come to the dance tonight." Amie explained.

"Oh, that makes sense," Emma commented. "By the way, how are the two of you doing?"

"Really well," Amie confided. "I know this sounds crazy but I am pretty sure he is 'the one.' We really vibe well together and we even look a little bit alike."

"That wouldn't surprise me at all," Kendi said, smiling. "I think good relationships start with being just friends first."

That comment launched a lively conversation between the three girls about the merits of guy friends versus boyfriends. Amie loved every minute of her time hanging out with Emma and Kendi as they walked the familiar road to the lake. Amie noted the pretty fall trees as they walked and reminisced about the great times they had, along with Hope, over the past summer. Kendi and Emma had both become Christians during the summer and they enjoyed doing Bible studies with Aunty Nola. Every now and again, over the course of the summer, Aunty Nola designated a special evening where the girls would discuss things that had been bothering them that they might need help to figure out. Amie really missed these special times.

The topic changed to Emma and Ryan, along with Emma's hope that they might progress in their relationship this weekend. Amie knew that Kendi had attended her own homecoming dance the previous weekend with Ryan, so she imagined that continuing this conversation might prove to be a little awkward. Amie was glad when they started discussing their dresses. She was relieved to know that they all had different styles and colors, and no one was duplicating each other. They talked about Hope's dress and how she was able to borrow from Amie's friend Julie.

Amie then told them how well Hope had adjusted to life in Chelan. "She seems really happy," she confirmed. "She has a lot of friends on her soccer team, and she is a lot more outgoing and confident than at the beginning of summer. The move has been good for her and hanging out with Aunty Nola has been an amazing opportunity for her and her mom when she comes on weekends. Hope doesn't have any grandparents, and Aunty Nola has taken both of them under her wing. You know Hope became a Christian, right?"

The girls chatted enthusiastically about this news. They were all excited that Hope was able to move to Chelan and spend more time with Aunty Nola.

They saw the crowd gathering at the sporting goods store, so they walked across the street.

"Oh, there's Hope! Looks like they are about to start!"

The Chamber of Commerce president kicked off the ribbon cutting by thanking them for coming, introducing himself, and congratulating Joe on his boat rental business and the successful acquisition of the sporting goods store. The mayor came up and read a proclamation declaring Everything Outdoors Sporting Goods as Chelan's Business of the Day.

The prizes were awarded to Mr. and Mrs. Arnold for winning the jingle and logo contests, then everyone clapped. After the dismissal, they sent everyone in to check out the store and grab some cake. The girls waited for it to be less crowded before they went inside. Emma went up to talk to the chamber president.

Amie watched Emma bravely march up to the chamber president and admired her initiative. She shared that trait with Emma because she was also bold when it came to things she was passionate about. Amie knew that if she had a chance to meet a clothing designer or someone in the fashion industry, she would do the same thing.

"It looks like the crowd is clearing! Let's go get some cake!" Emma suggested.

The girls walked around the store, hoping to see something that would make sense for them to buy. Amie found a pink camouflage-pattern t-shirt that she liked and got in line to purchase it. Emma wanted to get something at a reasonable price point, so she found a notebook with nature scenes on it. Kendi bought a package of colored golf balls with the brand new Everything Outdoors logo already printed on them for her dad.

When they got to the counter, they asked Hope when she thought she would be home to get ready.

"I'll take off in a little while," Hope replied. "It is slowing down here. I'll text you when I am leaving and find out where you are."

Amie was happy to see that all their parents were hanging out by the cake table with shopping bags in their hands. It was fun that all their parents had become friends, just like they had become friends. The girls told their parents that they were going to go back and start getting ready.

The girls walked back to the house and Amie grabbed her car and went home to do her nails and get everything she needed to get ready for the dance with the other girls. She came back about an hour later and the girls showed each other their dresses.

I can't wait until pictures!" Emma clapped her hands in delight.

"I know. I think the best part of homecoming is seeing all the pretty dresses," Amie stated. "Oh, and the guys in their fancy tuxes, too. This is going to be so much fun!"

****

Later that day, Emma, Kendi, Amie, and Hope busied themselves dressing and doing their hair and makeup, with their moms hovering around *oooo*ing and *ahh*ing over all the dresses. Hope had a long, lime green dress that looked beautiful on her. Her mom curled her hair and brushed it out into beachy waves, and she looked legit like a model. Kendi's blue dress looked amazing on her and contrasted beautifully with her long, wavy red hair.

Amie's off-the-shoulder dress was an striking fuchsia color and her lipstick and nail polish were a sparkly pink/purple that matched the dress. Amie was pleased with how her dress looked on her, and she round brushed her hair to give it more body and was happy with the result. She put on more makeup than usual, so it would look good in the formal pictures.

At 4:45, the girls went downstairs and went out to The Guesthouse's picturesque back yard, and the parents got started with the photo shoot before the boys arrived. The boys showed up promptly at five, and corsages and boutonnières were exchanged. All four couples got together for the group photos.

Amie's heart skipped a beat when she saw Josh in his tux. She was officially smitten, she realized. It felt good to be dating a college boy, especially one as attractive as Josh. When she attached his boutonnière to his lapel, Amie caught a whiff of his fragrant cologne, and she melted all over again. Her dad took a few pictures of Josh and Amie with the orchard in the background.

It was soon time to head over to the restaurant, so they went out to their cars and headed over there. At Stillwaters, Ryan and Emma sat near Josh and Amie, and the four of them had fun talking about Josh's experiences at the University of Washington. They thoroughly enjoyed their delicious dinners but had no room for dessert.

After dinner, they headed to the dance. The community center was hosting the homecoming dance, and it was beautifully decorated with green and silver metallic streamers, confetti, and photo backdrops. Amie loved how fancy it was.

Amie was surprised to discover that Josh loved dancing as much as she did. They stayed out on the dance floor through several sets of music, including about four slow songs. She loved dancing the slow songs in Josh's arms. He was so handsome, and he seemed so attentive to her. During one of the slower numbers, Josh told her that she looked absolutely beautiful. She melted under that compliment and hoped the song would never end. Of course, it ended, and once the fast songs picked back up, they put their swing dance skills into play again.

Amie looked around at one point and realized none of their friends were dancing. She told Josh they should probably take a break and hang out with their friends, and she led him off the dance floor. They found their friends and sat in the two remaining seats at their table.

"What shall we do after this?" Amie asked energetically.

"The coffee shop is open late tonight," Ben replied. "My brother Joseph is in charge, and one of the other baristas agreed to come in tonight, so we could get coffees. My brother might be persuaded to break out the karaoke machine. I told a few people, but I only mentioned it to people that I'm sure won't be partiers."

"Cool! It will be like summer nights!" Kendi exclaimed.

"But we're dressed a lot better," Ben confirmed.

Just then, the band announced that everyone needed to be on the dance floor for the next song.

"One last set before we go?" Amie begged. Everyone followed Amie and Josh as they led them to the dance floor for some fun and lively dancing. After a few fast songs, the band announced that the last number would be a slow song to end the evening. Josh drew Amie into his arms and Amie cuddled up to him during the slow song and breathed in the aroma of his cologne. *I can't believe Josh chose me to be his girlfriend. I'm so lucky!*

The group headed to Brandon's Coffee and Bakehop, where several other couples had already grabbed tables. Ben pulled a couple tables together to make room for their group. The girls gave their coffee orders to their dates, and the guys picked them up when their names were called.

Kendi and Ben sang a duet that they did this summer after much encouragement from Emma and Hope. Ryan sang "Sweet Caroline" which was well received.

Amie thought it would be really fun to do a group song so she tried to convince her friends to do an all-girls number. With some cajoling, Kendi and Emma agreed to do it, as did Hannah and a couple other girls from school. Hope was reluctant, but Amie talked her into being part of the performance, so Hope agreed to join the group. The girls sang "All the Single Ladies." Judging by the reaction from the guys in the audience, the performance was a success even though it was spur of the moment. When they were finished, they received rousing applause.

After a while, the coffee shop closed for the night, and Josh and Amie said goodnight to the others and got in his car. He asked her if she would like to go for a moonlit walk on the lake path. Amie considered it for a split second before she answered.

"Of course," Amie responded with a big smile. She was kind of hoping that they would hold hands for the first time tonight. As they drove the short distance to the lake, he joked with her about her "All the Single Ladies" number.

"Was that a message to me?" he teased.

Amie could feel herself turning red. That was 100% not her intention when she initiated that song. She was just thinking of a well-known song for a group of girls to perform on the fly. *Oh no, what did I do?*

She forced a laugh. "No! I was just trying to think of a fun song for girls that everyone would know. I'm a long way from being old enough to get engaged!" she replied.

"I was just joking," he explained. "You girls did great! We were all dying, it was so funny!" Amie felt relieved with that explanation.

They parked by the resort and walked on their familiar walking path. This time, he took her hand as they walked. Amie did not resist. She had been waiting for this moment, and she loved the way her small hand felt in his larger hand. She felt safe and treasured.

As they walked along, he asked if she had fun tonight.

"Oh my goodness, yes!" she assured him. They came to the park bench and sat down. "Did you have fun coming back to a high school dance?" she asked.

"Yes, but only because my date was the cutest girl there *and* the best dancer," he replied. Then he looked at her and said, "Correction, only because my *girlfriend* was totally the cutest girl there and definitely the best dancer."

Amie let that sink in. Her head was spinning with how great it felt to be called his girlfriend. She felt his hand cup her chin and lift it as he leaned in to kiss her.

She jolted back, and he looked at her in confusion. "Sorry, Josh! I was just surprised."

"Um, are we not allowed to kiss?" he asked, sounding a little confused.

Amie didn't know how to respond. She wanted him to kiss her, but she also thought they should take it slowly, like they had been doing. She didn't want to make him mad, but she wanted to do the right thing. *Yikes, I need to say something fast, but what?*

She took a breath and said, "Josh, I totally want to kiss you, but I think we should wait because I think it would be easy to get carried away. How about if we limit it to just a goodnight kiss at my door, for now?"

He shrugged and said, "Sure, if that's what you want. I guess it's fine."

"Are you mad at me?" she asked.

"Never!" he assured her, standing up. He grabbed her hand and pulled her to her feet and didn't let go as they started walking back. "This is still okay, right?"

"More than okay," she murmured. They walked back to the car in relative silence. He opened the passenger door for her and helped her into the car.

When he pulled up to her driveway, he helped her out of the car and walked her to the door. "I don't have to kiss you if you don't want..." Josh began.

She grabbed both his hands, pulled him towards her, and tilted her face up toward him. He leaned down and gave her a quick kiss, then headed for the car.

"Thanks for taking me to the dance!" she called.

"It was fun!" he replied with a smile as he got in his car and drove away.

Amie went inside, and her parents were waiting up for her. "Did you have a great time, Honey?"

"Totally!" Amie replied. "Josh is a great dancer, and it was so fun to hang out with my summer friends."

"It was fun to see all of you Guesthouse Girls dressed up like Cinderella," her dad commented.

"Did you get some good pictures?" Amie asked.

"Yes! Tons. I'll finish editing them and show you in the morning." Her dad had recently purchased some editing software to use on photographs he took of the lake, and he was excited to have a new use for it.

"Okay! Goodnight, you guys!"

"Goodnight, Honey," Staci said.

"I'll get those pictures edited so you can share them with your friends tomorrow," Randy reiterated.

Amie floated up the stairs, still enchanted by the evening. She replayed everything in her mind as she tucked herself under her fluffy comforter. The fun of being with The Guesthouse Girls, the yummy dinner, the revelation that Josh loved to dance as much as she did, the amazing slow dances, the hilarious rendition of "All the Single Ladies," the moonlit walk, the awful moment when she pulled away from the most romantic thing she had ever experienced, and the way the date ended with a good-night kiss and Josh not being mad at her and accepting how she felt. She was blissfully happy and thanked God repeatedly for this once-in-a-lifetime, nearly-perfect date.

CHAPTER EIGHT

Formal Recap

All The Guesthouse Girls were at church the next day, and they sat together and babbled about the previous night before church started. After church, they went to the lobby and continued their conversation, giggling about their coffee shop Beyonce song.

"I'm thinking we can start a girl group like one of the ones from the 80s and 90s. Instead of being The Spice Girls, we will be The Guesthouse Girls," Emma joked.

"We might not get any bookings, but the practices would be fun!" Amie agreed with a laugh.

"I'll play keyboards," Kendi offered.

"We may need to stick to our day jobs," Hope deadpanned.

The would-be-band was disbanded when Emma and Kendi's parents broke into the impromptu planning session to reclaim their daughters and take them to their homes on opposite sides of the state. This led to lots of hugs and promises of texts and calls. When they had left, Hope and Amie helped Aunty Nola clean up, then said goodbye to each other and went home.

****

This week at school was going to be a doozy, especially because Amie didn't do much homework due to her busy weekend. She had a test coming up in history, so she opened her laptop and started reviewing her notes on World War II. *Yikes, this is just not my thing.*

Her thoughts kept going back to walking hand in hand on the beach path with Josh before his botched kiss attempt. She decided to get her other subjects taken care of and attack WWII last. She went over her English reading assignment, her Spanish verb conjugation homework, and her physics homework, and she felt caught up in every class except the dreaded report.

She wandered downstairs for a snack. There were fresh apples on the counter, and they led her to want to bake. She looked around for her mom and found her hard at work in her office.

"Hey, Mom, can I make an apple cake to bring to Bible study tonight?" she asked.

"Sure, Honey, there are some boxes in the garage. Use some granny smith and some honey crisp."

"That's what I was thinking, too" Amie replied.

She did an internet search for "apple cake," and she found a recipe that looked delicious and easy. She preheated the oven according to the directions, assembled the wet ingredients in the rotating mixer, and turned it on to blend. She stood on her tiptoes and pulled down a pretty blue mixing bowl out of one of the oak cabinets and blended the dry ingredients together, adding just a bit more cinnamon and cloves than the recipe called for. She folded the wet and dry ingredients together and scraped them into a pan she had lined with parchment paper. She put the pan in the oven and set the timer on the microwave. The recipe was a two-in-one deal that also included a glaze to pour over the cake. Amie glanced at the time display on her phone and decided not to bother with the glaze. When the cake had cooled, she thought it looked fluffy and smelled delicious and she knew her friends would love it.

As usual, Amie was pressed for time and she rushed upstairs to get ready for her Bible study. She was excited that Hope had joined the group, along with Lexi, Hailey, Amanda, and a couple of other girls named Bailey and Sunni. She knew that all the talk tonight would probably center on homecoming and not so much on the study, but she was pretty sure their leader would understand.

An hour later, Amie arrived at church, clutching a fabric carrying case that held the still-warm apple cake, a cooler with vanilla ice cream, little pink paper plates, and utensils for both serving and eating the dessert. The girls in the study were used to Amie bringing treats, and they looked on in anticipation as she spread everything out on a nearby table.

Hope walked in as Amie was getting everything set out. "What is that smell?!?" she exclaimed.

"It is probably the apple spice cake made with apples from The Guesthouse orchard," Amie informed her. "Are you hungry?"

Hope grinned. "Always!" The girls, including their leader Shanna, helped themselves to cake and ice cream and settled in to talk.

While they were devouring the freshly-baked cake, Shanna blurted, "Okay, out with it! I want to hear all about homecoming and see all the pictures!"

"Okay, I'll start," Amanda began. "Turns out Gabe is super funny, and we had a good time. It could not have been more different that what I expected. He is quiet in class, so I expected he would be that way in person, but he has an amazing personality, and we had so much fun. He kept me laughing all through dinner."

"I didn't see you at the dance," Amie remarked.

"I know. We didn't stay long. Neither of us really wanted to dance, so we hung around long enough to get pictures and say hi to a few people and then we went to a fancy party his parents were throwing at a winery for his aunt's anniversary. Everyone was dressed up there, so we fit in okay. It was fun to hang out with his family. Here are some pictures they took of us there, Amanda revealed, handing her phone to Hailey."

"You looked beautiful in that dress and you seem so comfortable together in these pictures. Are you going to start dating?" Hailey asked, continuing to flip through the photos.

"I think so. I guess we'll see if he asks me out again." Amanda answered.

"Wow, that dress was perfect!" Shanna commented.

"Well, I had help picking it out," Amanda confessed, looking at her shopping buddies.

"Who's next?" Shanna asked, eager for more homecoming tales.

One by one, the girls related their experiences and showed off their pictures. When it was Amie's turn, she repeated most of the same things Hope had shared, stopping her story after the coffee shop portion of the evening. Everyone loved the photos that her dad had taken and proudly edited, and both her boyfriend and fuchsia dress were properly gushed over. All the sharing took up most of their allotted time, but it was good group bonding, and no one was left out.

Shanna asked if anyone had any prayer requests or praises. Amie thought about asking for prayer about figuring out her boundaries with Josh, but she thought that was a little too personal. When it was her turn, she asked if they could pray about an unspoken request. They all agreed and had a time of prayer for both the praises and the requests that people had shared with the group. Amie thoroughly enjoyed their time together and was glad she had come.

On the way out, she pulled Hope aside. "It was fun to hang out with you this weekend! Looks like things are going well for you and Conner."

"Yeah, I actually am going to ice cream with him tonight, so I need to go home and get ready."

"Okay! Have fun!" Amie replied.

"See you in Spanish!" Hope called back to her as she left.

CHAPTER NINE

Snowy Montana

One lazy Saturday morning, early in November, Amie was at home with her mom, sitting on a comfy gray bar stool next to the expansive sparkly white marble countertop. She was finishing up a piece of French toast that her mom cooked, drizzled with some coconut syrup that was sent from her aunt Gail who lived on Maui.

Amie absently let her hand drift across the new, smooth countertop. About a year ago, Amie's parents had started much-needed renovation to their large lakeside house. They started in the living room and were working outward from there. So far, the living room, the kitchen, and family room had been completed, and, in a couple of weeks, the construction workers would be starting on the upstairs rooms. Amie's dad always liked to hire workers to do renovation projects this time of year because it was getting too cold and snowy for them to effectively do outdoor projects, and the guys were hungry for work. Construction projects created thick clouds of dusty air throughout the house, rendering the home uninhabitable, so Amie's dad Randy planned to start renovations on Friday before Thanksgiving week, and Amie and her parents would spend the week elsewhere to avoid breathing in the dust.

That day was approaching, and Amie scheduled today to completely pack up the stuff in her room to protect it from dust damage. She would also pack a few suitcases to take to wherever they were spending their days away from the house. They had taken to calling this time their "renovation vacation" or "reno-cation" for short. Amie wasn't sure where they were going to stay. Her dad and mom had kicked around some ideas, such as getting some rooms at The Guesthouse, staying at the resort, or staying at another property to get ideas for the Lakeside Resort. Amie liked the idea of staying in another property elsewhere, like in Arizona, for example. She was unashamedly a summer girl, and the cold weather got her down, even if she did enjoy changing out her wardrobes for fall, then winter. Her parents told her that they were not taking a trip to Arizona, especially when her dad had his hands full managing the reconstruction of the wing.

Amie's mom's phone rang from where it was plugged into a charger in the living room, and her mom scooted over to pick it up. She looked down and saw it was her sister calling from Maui. Maui was only two hours behind them this time of year, but Staci was still surprised to see her sister calling this early. "Hey, Gail! What's up?" Amie's mom greeted her sister.

Amie loved hearing from her Aunt Gail and hovered in closer, so she could hear what she had to say. "Hey, Staci, I got a call from the hospital. Apparently, Dad fell again, and this time, he hurt his leg, and he possibly sustained other injuries, too. He is in the hospital getting it taken care of. He may have fallen because his heart wasn't beating fast enough and he passed out. If that is the case, they might need to install a pacemaker. Supposedly, that is a fairly routine procedure, although it sounds like a big deal to me! I guess Dad put me down as his emergency contact because I am the older sister," she laughed. "I tried to call Dad, but he was sleeping. I guess one of us should go be with him in Montana, and you and Randy already spent all summer taking care of him, so I'll look into flights and let you know what I come up with."

"Okay..." Staci hesitated. "Did the hospital say how he was doing or give you any other details?"

"No, just that he fell and broke his leg and possibly a couple other bones, and they would know more later."

"Hmm...okay, call me back *before* you book your flights. I'll talk to Randy."

"Okay, love you, Sis!"

Amie was waving wildly to get her mom's attention. "Oh, Amie wants me to tell you that she loves you, too!"

"Hey, Princess!" Amie could dimly hear Aunt Gail yelling into the phone from where she stood across the room.

"Hi, Aunty Gail!" Amie called, walking closer so she would be heard.

"Okay, bye, Gail!" Staci ended the call. "I don't know why I didn't just put it on speaker," she commented.

"I was wondering that, too," Amie murmured under her breath. Then, louder, she asked, "How is Grandpa doing?"

"Amie, don't sass–I heard that. We don't know how Grandpa is doing for sure. I need to call your dad." With that, Staci touched her husband's name on her phone and he answered on the first ring. Again, Amie could hear the gist of her dad's side of the conversation without it being on speaker, and she wondered why her mom didn't just hit the speaker button.

"What's up?" Randy asked.

"Well, Gail just called and said the hospital called her, and Dad fell and is in the hospital now."

"Oh, no! Is he okay?" Randy asked.

"We just know that he fell at home, broke his leg, and maybe has other injuries. They think that his heart has been beating too slowly, causing him to pass out, and that's why he fell. The doctor thinks that they might need to put in a pacemaker, so this doesn't happen again in the future. Gail said she was going to look for flights, so she could go be with him since we stayed with him all summer when he was recovering from surgery, but I had a different idea," Staci ventured.

"Oh really? What's that? Does it involve me going to Montana in the winter?" Randy asked with hesitation, "Because I am pretty slammed here at work."

"Actually, no. I was going to suggest that we start the renovations on the house earlier than planned, Amie and I fly into Montana, and you can stay at an empty room at the resort."

Amie raised her eyebrows with interest. She wasn't sure how she felt about leaving school to go to snowy Montana right now, but it might actually be fun.

"Are you sure you want to do that, Honey?" Amie could barely hear her dad's voice coming out of her mom's phone.

"I think so," Staci answered. "I'll check out some flights and talk to Amie about it."

"Okay," Randy answered slowly, "It might be a good idea because we can get a jump on the remodeling. Let me know what you find out about flights."

"Okay, bye, Honey," Staci replied, ending the call.

Staci hung up. "What do you think, Amie?"

"I like the idea," Amie agreed. "I'll just need to talk to my teachers about getting work to do from Montana. I think it's possible. I've seen other kids get to do it."

"Okay. We'll call the school on Monday. Actually, it would be nice to fly out earlier if possible. I'll call your principal, Mr. Wilson, at home and ask him since this is kind of an emergency. But first, I need to check flights," she commented as she grabbed her phone and headed back to her office computer. Amie trailed behind her.

Staci pulled up flights to Missoula, Montana from both Seattle and Spokane, Washington. They could save about $200 each by flying out on Sunday instead of Monday and leaving out of Seattle instead of Spokane, although it was about a half-hour longer drive.

"Let's go out of Seattle, and we can use the money we save at Nordstrom," Amie suggested hopefully.

"Nice try, Amie-girl. I don't envision much shopping on this trip. Keep in mind, we are spending a lot of money on this renovation, and *somebody* needs to go to college in a couple years."

"I suppose you're right," Amie agreed.

Just then, the phone rang. Amie could tell from her mom's voice that it was Gail. This time, Staci pushed the speakerphone option.

"Hi, Gail, you're on speaker with Amie and me."

"Oh cool!" Gail started. "Okay, here's the deal. I can get a flight out, but not until Monday, and it's $1200."

"Yikes!" Staci replied. "The high cost of paradise!"

"Yes. Apparently, there is not a big demand from people wanting to travel from Hawaii to Missoula in the winter, and they really stick it to you."

"Wow. Seattle to Missoula is a third of that price."

"Why were you searching ?" Gail asked curiously.

"Well, Randy is doing some renovations on our house, and we are going to have to vacate the house anyway in the next couple of weeks, so I figured, if we have to leave anyway, maybe it makes sense to hang out with Dad a while. I'm going to call Amie's principal and make sure that it can be arranged."

"Are you sure?" Gail asked. "I don't want to duck out of my responsibility just because I live far away."

"No, it's cool," Staci answered. "Amie and I can deal with it this time, and you can just owe us," she joked.

"Done." Gail agreed. "I will definitely repay you for this! I'll also call in and check on you guys and Dad every day."

"Okay! Well, I got some arrangements to make, so I'm going to hang up now. Call me if you get any updates about Dad, and I'll let you know our flight plans."

Gail gave Staci the phone number for the nurses' station in her dad's area of the hospital, and the two said I love you's and goodbyes, then hung up.

While they were talking, Amie had searched several airlines and found an even better deal on flights the next morning out of Seattle. They decided to leave tonight and spend the night in Seattle, assuming they were able to reach Mr. Wilson and he could clear Amie's extended absence from school. So, Amie kept their potential flights unbooked on the computer and went upstairs to pack in earnest for what could possibly be a month-long stay. She figured she would need about three suitcases because winter clothing was bulky. She selected three of the largest ones they had from their storage area and proceeded to pack. When Amie's mom came upstairs to tell her about her talk with Mr. Wilson, she shook her head no and slid her flattened hand across her throat in a gesture that corresponded with her words, "Not happening."

"What, did Mr. Wilson say no?"

"No, he said yes, and he said the school will be unlocked this afternoon for a rec league game, and you should bring all your books with you. We can coordinate with each teacher individually to have them email your assignments. He said the toughest class to make up work in will be physics. I told him that your grandpa was a physics teacher for years, he would run the labs with you, and you could provide pictures, or video, whatever proof was appropriate. He was satisfied with that answer."

"Oh, good," Amie breathed a sigh of relief. "Wait— why were you shaking your head no?"

"Because you're only going to bring one large suitcase and one carry-on. It's not a fashion show. We're staying at grandpa's house, and he has a washer and dryer, so you'll have plenty of clothes. I'm not paying extra to bring your whole wardrobe," she smiled. Amie nodded, then headed upstairs to rework her packing situation.

Okay, I guess if we are missing something, we can just buy it there, Amie thought, excitement building a little at the thought of going shopping. She even had a fleeting thought that she should purposely leave something behind so they could have an excuse to shop, but her logical side took over just in time.

When Amie finally finished packing, she padded downstairs in her stocking feet. Staci was on the phone with Randy, filling him in on the details. She got off the phone and announced, "Dad is on his way home, so he can hang out with us before we need leave for Seattle. I booked the flights, and I also booked a hotel for the night near the airport."

"Oh, good, I put an extra suitcase in your room," Amie grinned sheepishly. "Do you need help packing?"

"No, that's okay," Staci answered.

"Have you heard anything about Grandpa?" Amie wrinkled her face with concern.

"No, I was going to wait until Dad got home and call then. Oh, I hear him now." Staci and Amie heard the purr of the garage opening and rushed to greet him.

Amie's dad Randy threw an arm around each of them and pulled them into a group hug.

"Any news on your Dad, Honey?" he directed his gaze toward Staci.

"Nothing yet. I was waiting for you to come home before I called," she said, then sniffed, her concern for her father evident.

"Okay, well, let's do it," he replied, picking up her phone and handing it to his wife.

She pressed the necessary keys to get her to the nurses' station and put the phone on speaker and soon, they could hear someone named Lauren answering the phone. Staci identified herself and asked for an update.

"He is resting comfortably," Lauren explained. "The doctor has been by, and he has ordered a bunch of tests. Actually, it looks like they are about to take him to one of his tests now, so you'll probably need to talk with him a little later. It looks like they are probably going to be installing a pacemaker at some point to regulate his heart. If they do, it will be a fairly routine procedure."

"Okay, please let him know that I called. My daughter and I will be coming tomorrow, but don't tell him yet, since we don't know exactly what time we will arrive, and we don't want him to worry if it takes longer than we expect."

"Sounds good," Lauren agreed. "Mum's the word."

"When do you think they will put the pacemaker in, assuming it's needed?" Staci asked.

"Possibly later in the day tomorrow, so you might make it in time." They talked more then hung up.

"Well, that sounded promising," Randy began tentatively.

"Yeah," Staci replied. "Amie and I are about ready to get on the road as soon as I throw some things in a suitcase. We'll stop by the school and grab her books, and when we get to Seattle, we'll shop a little bit before we go to our hotel and then get on our flight in the morning." Amie's ears perked up when she heard that her mom changed her tune about Seattle shopping. She kind of assumed that would be the case because her mom loved to shop almost as much as Amie did.

"That's what I figured," Randy stated with a grin toward Amie. "What can I do to help you girls get out the door?"

"You can come help me pack," Staci directed. "Then, I can spend a little more time with you before I have to go."

The two of them went upstairs and gathered some things for the suitcase. Amie stayed downstairs and texted some of her friends, including Josh.

Josh took a while to answer back, but Amie knew he had a lot of group projects for his classes, and Sunday afternoons tended to be busy for him, when he wasn't in Chelan. He had told her in a recent text that he was going to come home a lot less often than he had planned because his parents had told him that it was looking like it would be a worse winter than expected, and they didn't want him to drive on icy roads for almost four hours, twice each weekend that he came home. Amie was seriously disappointed when she first heard that news, but she understood and wanted him to be safe. She also wanted him to have weekends available to complete his homework. Josh had said that his boss at the restaurant was fine with working with his schedule, especially since they didn't have enough hours for everybody in the winter anyway. Josh had told Amie that they would video chat more to make up for him not coming home as much.

Amie's mom and dad then came downstairs. Randy was hauling Staci's suitcase, and Staci was holding the handle of an attractive matching carry-on bag. "I think we're ready," Staci announced to Amie.

"Me, too," Amie agreed. "Oh, wait!" She ran upstairs and grabbed another pair of black and white earrings and a basic black turtleneck shirt from her winter wardrobe. She rushed downstairs and placed them in her carry-on bag and panted, "Okay, mom. I'm ready, too!"

Randy loaded their bags in the car and waved goodbye when they drove away. They stopped by the school, and Amie collected the necessary books from her locker. *Oh, no, these are heavy. Looks like we will have some overweight baggage charges!* she thought to herself. She stuffed all the books she thought she would need into her backpack and hustled to the parking lot and hopped in the front seat. "Let's get to Seattle!" she encouraged.

On the way to the hotel, they talked about the remodel of their home, how things were going at the resort, Amie's recent mid-quarter report card, and how they thought Grandpa was doing. The time passed quickly, and they drove straight to the hotel where they would be staying, checked in, and put their luggage in their rooms. At this point, it was dinner time. Amie was really tired, and she actually just wanted to lay down on her comfortable bed. She mentioned that to her mom.

"I feel the same way. Let's just order a pizza or room service and call it good. We can't fit anything more in our bags, anyway. We can probably shop after the flight back here." The two of them selected some delicious-sounding salads from the room service menu, then settled in and watched a Hallmark Christmas movie before calling it a night.

****

The next morning was a rude awakening when the phone alarm went off. Amie drug herself out of bed and saw that her mom had already showered and was doing her devotional. Amie stumbled in to take her shower and put on some warm clothes for the flight to Montana. One glance at the weather app on her phone assured her to dress extra warm because it would be frigid when they arrived. She pulled out the black turtleneck she had added at the last minute and put it under the wool sweater she was planning to wear. She blew her hair dry, and, not liking the humidity's frizzy effect on her hair, she shrugged and grabbed a rarely used hair tie from her accessory bag and opted for a high ponytail and no makeup. She did take a moment and put on the black and white earrings which would take center-stage with her ears exposed.

"Time to move, Amie-girl!" her mom called.

"I'm ready," Amie sighed, not excited to face the rain that was pounding down on the pavement outside her window. After that would be a crowded airport, followed by freakishly cold Montana winter weather. Amie yawned, still half-asleep, and obediently followed her mother to the lobby. From there, they caught a shuttle and arrived at the airport in plenty of time to clear security, walk toward their gate, and grab some coffee and breakfast to go. They sat side by side wordlessly in the black airport chairs until it was time to line up to load the plane. Amie dragged her bag behind her and was glad when she was seated by the window, so she could lean her head against it and sleep. She vaguely heard the safety briefing before she fell asleep, completely missing the plane's take-off.

She woke up from her nap just before they were about to land from their hour and a half flight.

"Good morning, sunshine!" her mom Staci whispered. "You must have been tired!"

"I was," Amie agreed. "But now, I'm rested. Look how pretty the trees look covered in snow!" Amie gazed out her window in child-like delight.

"And … she's back! Amazing what a little nap can do." Staci grinned at Amie's transformation back to her perky self.

By the time they had received their bags from baggage claim and picked up a rental car, they were ready for lunch. Staci was glad to see that despite the large snowdrifts, the roads were relatively clear. They went through a hamburger drive-through on the way to the hospital.

When they arrived at the hospital, the nurse on duty ushered them into Grandpa Peterson's room. Amie saw a big white dry-erase board across from the foot of the bed with Grandpa Peterson's name and various numbers. She also noticed that under "Family" was the name Staci, along with her mom's cell phone number. Grandpa Peterson was sleeping when they walked in, and Amie was surprised how much he had changed since the last time she had seen him. He looked much older than he did last Christmas. He had much less hair, and he seemed a lot thinner. Soon, her grandpa opened his eyes.

"Well, aren't you two a sight for sore eyes," Grandpa joked. "Where's Randy?"

"Hi, Dad. We left him at home to get some work done on our renovation," Staci answered, bending toward the bed for a hug. "How are you? What do the doctors say?"

Amie distracted her grandpa momentarily with a hug and then he turned his attention back to Staci. "I broke a few bones in my leg and one in my wrist, no big deal and definitely not worth you guys coming all the way here in the snow!"

"We wanted to come," Amie spoke up cheerfully. "I never get to see you!"

"Well, in that case, I'm glad you're here. You are my favorite grandchild, you know! Just don't tell the others," he joked.

"Grandpa, I'm your *only* grandchild," Amie reminded him with a laugh.

"Well, then, you're definitely my favorite!" he reiterated. One of the nurse's aides had brought another chair near the hospital bed, so both Amie and her mom could sit down. "Aren't you taking physics this year?"

Amie smiled. "Yes, Grandpa."

"Why are you skipping the most important class of your high school career to sit around a hospital in Montana?" he demanded.

"Says the retired physics teacher," Staci responded. "Amie will be doing schoolwork while we are in town."

Grandpa made a face at his daughter and turned back to Amie. "What else have you been doing, Amie?"

141

"Well, I had homecoming, and that was fun," Amie began.

"I know, your mom sent me a picture of you and a college boy. I think he is a little old for you. Watch out for that one," Grandpa Peterson looked at Staci this time.

"Oh, Grandpa, he is fine. We work together at the resort," Amie jumped in. Changing the subject, she added, "Well, I've also been going to my Bible study group at church."

"Hmm...you guys are still doing the church thing?" he replied skeptically.

"Of course, we are," Amie replied. "What about you?"

"No church, not for me," Grandpa Peterson replied. "See those mountains out there? That's is my church, and that's my Bible. I don't need a preacher and a building to be spiritual."

"Oh, Dad, we've talked about this before," Staci protested. "The only way to Heaven is through Jesus, not a mountain. The Bible tells us in Romans to worship the Creator, not created things."

"Well, I know you two did not come to argue with me, so let's talk about Amie some more. How did you like staying in that boarding house this summer?"

"It's called 'The Guesthouse,' Grandpa, and it was awesome! The other girls and I got along great all summer, and we are still in contact. One of them actually got to stay in Chelan year-round, and the other two text with us frequently."

"Well, that's good, Sunshine. When you get a good friend, hang on to them, they are golden!" Grandpa stated. "Except that college boy. He's trouble."

Amie looked at her mom helplessly. Her mom returned her gaze and gave a slight shake of her head as if to say, *Don't argue with him. He doesn't know anything about Josh.*

A pretty young nurse with long blonde hair then came into the room. "Hi, I'm Lauren! I talked with you on the phone, if you are Staci," she said warmly with a wave in Staci's direction.

"Yes, that's me. Thanks for taking care of my dad. Has he been a good patient?"

"Yes, for the most part." She smiled. "He is going to head into surgery to get the pacemaker installed, so we are going to have to break up this happy reunion for a little while. If you need lunch, or you have somewhere to go, you'll have some time for that now. He'll be back in the room in about an hour or two. Wait for a call from the recovery room nurse, so you'll know he is back in the room."

"Okay, Dad," Staci agreed. She went over to the bed and gave her dad a hug and kissed his cheek. "We'll be back in an hour. Anything we can get for you?"

"Yes, get me a couple cold beers," he joked.

"No, really, is there anything you'd like us to bring from your house?" she persisted.

"Nah, I can't think of anything. Just come back. I love you, Staci. Thanks for being here."

"No problem, Dad! I love you, too!"

"As for you, little squirt," Amie's grandpa began, looking at her. "Come give me a hug."

Amie did as he requested and leaned over and gave him an awkward hug, trying to avoid the hospital wires. She leaned her head onto his chest.

"You're a sweetheart, Amie. I'm so glad you came here with your mom."

"Me, too," Amie agreed. "I've missed you!"

"I've missed you, too. We'll see you in a while," he said, shooing them out.

Amie whispered to her mom as they got into the elevator and rode it down to where their car was parked: "Grandpa looked a lot different than he did last Christmas."

"I know, he looked a lot different than when we left him at the end of summer," Staci remarked. "Maybe it's just because he is in the hospital. Once we get him home, we can cook for him and restore his strength."

"Yeah, that will be good," Amie agreed.

"What shall we do while we wait?" Staci asked.

Amie got a mischievous look in her eye. "Remember that place that had that pie? Is that still in business?"

Staci grinned, "Yep, I may have gained a couple pounds this summer because of that place. Your dad and I had to limit ourselves to one slice a week."

"So...can we go there?" Amie coaxed.

"Sure, why not?" Staci agreed. "But remember, no more than once a week, so you better savor it!"

A few minutes later they pulled into the snow-covered parking lot, and Staci parked the car. Amie looked up and saw the familiar yellow awning with a sketch of a pie with a pie server emblazoned on it. They got out, and the brunette hostess seated them at a table large enough for four by the window and handed them each a menu that had seen better days.

"Are you ladies here for lunch or for pie?" she asked.

"Pie," Amie answered with a sparkle in her blue eyes.

"Very good," the hostess answered. "Marcie will be with you in just a moment."

Amie and her mom were the only customers in the restaurant except for a pair of older gentlemen across the restaurant who were playing cards and had their canes leaned against the table and a middle-aged couple bundled up in winter clothing who were both munching on sandwiches and drinking hot chocolate.

Amie looked at the extensive pie menu and had to make the tough decision between key lime and chocolate silk pie. As she was agonizing over the decision, her mom announced, "I'm getting chocolate silk."

"Oh, good, then I'll get key lime, and we can share," Amie determined, and her mom nodded in agreement.

Marcie, a woman about sixty-years-old with long, salt and pepper hair and a faded red apron came over to take their order. Staci ordered for the two of them, then asked for a couple waters. Less than five minutes later, Marcie returned with two generous slices of pie, both coated with swirls of real whipping cream. Amie and her mom grabbed their forks and sampled each other's pie, as well as their own, and pronounced them equally delicious. They savored the creamy goodness and the impossibly flaky crust until every last crumb had been consumed.

Staci paid for the pie and laughed quietly about why the two gentlemen that were playing cards were not overweight since it looked like they hung out at the pie shop every day, based on their familiarity with Marcie and the hostess. After a while of watching the two gentlemen play, Amie had an idea.

She asked the hostess, "Do you guys have any cards?"

"Do you mean playing cards?" the hostess asked with a smile. "If so, yes we do." She reached under her cubby and pulled out a well-worn deck of playing cards that had a photo of sprawling Montana wheat fields on the back of them.

"Oh, thank you so much!" Amie and her mom both exclaimed.

Amie dealt the cards, and she taught her mom a game that she had learned at a church retreat. Before they knew it, they had played about five rounds, and a couple hours had passed. They were wondering why they hadn't received a phone call yet, and Staci checked her phone to make sure that the ringer was on and that she hadn't missed a call.

While she was looking at it, her phone rang. She looked down and saw the number had a local area code 406 and knew that it must be the hospital calling.

"Hello?" she answered.

Amie was shuffling the cards and wasn't paying too much attention because she expected that it was a routine call telling them that her grandpa was in recovery and would be back in his room momentarily. She heard her mom make a sharp gasp. She turned to see the blood drain from Staci's face.

"We'll be right in," Staci responded and hung up the phone. She grabbed Amie by the arm, leaving the shuffled cards on the table, and rushed across the parking lot towards the car and explained, "Grandpa took a turn for the worse, and he's in the ICU room 440 now." Amie wanted to know more, but the look on her mom's face let her know this was definitely no time for questions.

They got back to the hospital and made a beeline through the automatic glass door.

As they rushed into the lobby, Staci looked at the sweet lady manning the information desk and demanded, "Where is room 440?"

The lady pointed to the elevator and said, "Go up to the fourth floor and take a left through the double doors. You'll see it on the left." Staci nodded in appreciation as she hurried toward the elevator.

They reached the elevator and rode in silence. When the elevator door opened, they took off like a shot and reached Grandpa Peterson's room in record time. The curtain was pulled around the bed, but Staci did not let that stop her. She slipped through the gap where the curtains met and joined a couple nurses, as well as a physician. Amie could see her grandpa through the crack in the curtain. His face was white, and his eyes were blank. He had a tube going down his throat that Amie knew from TV shows must be a ventilator. There was a large monitor with multiple waveforms in various colors marching across the dark screen. Amie did not have a clue what it meant. She listened to the ventilator rhythmically breathing for her grandpa and was overwhelmed by all of it, especially considering her grandpa was laughing and joking just a little while ago.

"What happened?" Staci demanded as Amie listened in from behind the curtain.

"His heart stopped during the procedure. It is possible that a blood clot broke loose," the doctor responded. "We did some CT scans and discovered blot clots in both his lungs and his brain. We have him on a ventilator now, so he is alive, but there is no evidence of brain function. It appears that he had a massive stroke."

Staci sank into a nearby chair, seemingly unable to comprehend what she had just been told. Amie was in a similar state of shock. Her body felt totally numb and she had no words; just confusion.

"But he was fine a little while ago," Amie protested, finding her voice.

"Yes, this happened suddenly," the doctor agreed.

"Is he going to get better?" Staci spoke in a voice barely louder than a whisper.

The doctor looked at her with compassion and uttered softly, "I really don't think so, but we are doing everything we can. His systems appear to be shutting down."

"Please fight for him!" Staci begged. "He isn't ready to die. He wants to live!"

"We're doing everything we can," the doctor repeated softly. "Unfortunately, the damage from a stroke of this scale is almost always irreversible. Is there anyone you need to call?"

Amie's mom was lost in the moment and had forgotten that they should let others know.

"Do you want me to call Dad or Aunt Gail?" Amie asked, her voice shaky.

"I better do it. I'll step into the waiting room. Do you want to wait here or come with me?"

Amie glanced at the nurses busily adjusting wires and decided that her mom needed her support more than her grandpa did at this point, and she was scared to be in the room right now without her mom. "I'll come with you."

One of the nurses, whose name tag said Kate, escorted the two of them as they went to a special private waiting room, and they went about making their calls. Because the room was empty, Staci turned on the speaker phone.

They called Gail in Maui first since it was the most critical to let her know what was going on. The two of them had a short discussion, and Gail gave Staci permission to do what she thought was best if any decisions needed to be made. They hung up quickly after Amie and her mom agreed to frequent updates.

Next, Staci called her husband and explained the situation. He told her he would be praying, and he would arrange a flight.

Staci advised him to hold off. "Honey, there is nothing you can do here. Let's just wait until we have a better idea which direction this is going."

"Are you sure? I am prepared to drop everything and get there. I can fly or drive, whichever would be quicker."

"No, just wait. I have Amie here, and Gail might fly in, too, depending."

"Okay, Honey. Keep me informed. How are you?"

"I'm good, but I feel like we need to get back in there," she replied.

"Fair enough. I'll let you go. Talk soon! Love you both!"

Amie and Staci hurried back to the room. Their nurse, Kate, looked at them sadly. "We called the chaplain, and we believe he is going to pass soon. He had a 'Do Not Resuscitate' order, so we will need to abide by his wishes and remove the ventilator soon. If you want to hold his hands, it is okay."

Amie was terrified to touch him, and she was in a state of shock. She knew that however she was feeling, her mom was likely feeling much worse since it was her own dad. Staci went to the right side of the bed and held her dad's cold, limp hand. Her shaky voice tried to encourage him to keep fighting because he had a lot to live for. Amie stood behind Staci, holding her mom's arm as she listened to her helpless pleas, and she tried to be as supportive as she could. Amie had tears streaming down her face. She'd been so looking forward to seeing her grandpa on this trip, and already, after talking to him a few minutes, he might be taken from them.

She prayed silently as she stood there. *Lord, I don't want Grandpa to die before he accepts Your gift of salvation. Please, even now in his unconscious state, give him another chance. Please let him live!*

When she had her eyes closed, apparently someone had dropped off some blueberry muffins, a carafe of coffee, and a pitcher of ice water for them. Eating was the last thing on their mind at that point, but Amie robotically poured a cup of coffee for herself and her mom in response to how cold it felt in the room.

A man in a clerical collar entered the room. He introduced himself as Harold, the hospital chaplain. He asked if they needed to call anyone to let them know that the ventilator was being removed. Staci nodded wordlessly. Amie held out her hand in a wordless gesture to make the phone calls to Gail and her dad. Staci handed Amie the phone.

"Hi, Aunt Gail," Amie started once her aunt had answered. "Grandpa had something in his chart that said that he wanted to die naturally, so they need to remove the ventilator. Do you want me to put the phone by his ear, so you can talk to him? They said that he may not be able to hear us, but maybe he can."

Gail responded in the affirmative, and Amie held the phone to her grandpa's ear. She saw a glimmer of change on his face when Gail began to speak, but it may have just been hopefulness on Amie's part. When Amie thought Gail had finished talking, Amie put the phone to her own ear and asked if she had finished.

She could hear Gail crying before she finally whispered, "Yes, Amie. Thank you so much for making that happen for me."

Amie said that she would put her on speaker so she could hear the chaplain's prayer. Amie and her mom stood next to her grandpa as the chaplain prayed, giving thanks to God for His kindness to create life and for giving Mr. Peterson such a rich time on earth with so many memories for so many years. He thanked God for His kindness to make salvation available through His Son and asked God for comfort for the family. When he finished, the nurses sent Amie and Staci out of the room so they could remove the equipment.

They sat in their waiting room, and Staci updated Randy about what was going on. A few minutes later, another nurse, whose nametag said Katie came and ushered Amie and Staci back into the room. As they were walking back into the room, Amie had a random thought about how odd it was to have two nurses with such similar names. *I wonder if that gets confusing when they are working together?* She refocused her thoughts, and, as they entered the room, she was relieved to see that not only was the ventilator removed, but so was all the wires and monitors, and Grandpa Peterson looked more like the guy who was teasing her about dating a college guy a few hours ago.

Kate, the first nurse, put her hand on Staci's shoulder. "Go ahead and hold your dad's hand. We're told that hearing is the last sense to go so he may actually hear you if you talk or sing to him. I'll leave you guys alone with him."

Staci connected Gail on a video call so they could witness their dad's final moments together. Harold held the phone for Staci, so Gail could see both her sister and her father. Once again, Staci held his hand, and Amie hovered close, praying silently. Staci told her dad it was okay to let go and reach for the hand of Jesus.

"Daddy, you are still alive, and you can still make the choice. Choose the gift Jesus offers, and you will live forever in Heaven, and we will be reunited together someday." Then, turning to Harold, the chaplain, helplessly, she said, "I don't know that he heard me."

Harold looked at her quietly. "You don't know that he didn't hear you, either." Harold noticed Grandpa Peterson's breathing slow down significantly and said, "It won't be long now." The chaplain looked at Amie, who had been trying to keep it together. "Do you want to wait in the waiting room?" Amie gave her mom a frantic look that told her she would do whatever she wanted her to do.

"Amie, go ahead. I have Gail here on the phone, and I have Harold. Go to the waiting room and call Daddy."

"Are you sure?" Amie gulped back a sob.

"Yes, go, Honey. There is nothing you can do here."

Amie scooted out to the waiting room and called her dad. The two of them prayed together, and it wasn't long before Harold and Staci emerged from the room together. Staci nodded, and Amie knew Grandpa Peterson had passed. Amie handed the phone to Staci so she could talk to her husband, and Amie's tears started to flow. Staci told Randy that she would call him when they got to Grandpa's house.

Staci and Amie said goodbye to Harold and received hugs from the nurses, Kate and Katie, and left the waiting area with the bag of Grandpa Peterson's personal belongings that was retrieved for them.

On the way toward the elevator, Staci told Amie, "I'd like to let our nurse Lauren know what happened."

"Okay," Amie agreed. "She was so nice."

They rode the elevator down to the floor of Grandpa Peterson's first room. As the door opened, they saw that their nurse Lauren was about to enter it with some colleagues. They were each carrying a notebook, and it looked as if they were headed to a meeting. When Lauren saw Staci and Amie, she stepped back. She let the others know that she would take another elevator and asked Staci and Amie about Grandpa.

"He didn't make it," Staci reported, her face white and holding back tears.

"I'm so sorry," Lauren responded. "How are you?"

"We're doing okay," Staci responded as Amie nodded in agreement, feeling completely numb.

"I'm so glad that the two of you had a chance to see him before he passed," Lauren responded. "I could tell that you all loved each other a great deal. I heard you talking to him about your faith and I will be praying for you as you grieve."

"Thank you," Staci responded. "We did … well, we just wanted to let you know, and it looks like you were heading to a meeting, so we won't keep you."

The nurse gave Amie and Staci a quick hug and said goodbye as she slipped into an elevator that was heading upwards. Moments later, an elevator door opened that was going downward, and Amie and her mom moved forward robotically into it.

****

They went back to Grandpa's house and sat down in the living room. Staci insisted that Amie lie down and try to take a nap while she figured out next steps. Amie dutifully went back to the room she typically stayed in when she visited, curled up on the bed, and texted Josh. She hadn't thought of him at all during the crisis, and she wanted to let him know what was going on.

She knew he was probably in his dorm working on homework since it was Sunday evening. She texted, "Hey, Josh," and waited for a response. After about ten minutes she texted again: "Hey, could you call me asap?" Still nothing. She waited fifteen minutes and tried calling, and it went straight to voicemail. Amie left a message for him to please call her back soon because it was urgent. Amie fell asleep waiting for him.

She woke up a couple hours later and padded out to the kitchen in some fuzzy pink socks that she retrieved from her carry-on bag. She noticed that her mom was sleeping on the couch, and she didn't want to awaken her. She tiptoed to the fridge to see what was in it. Nothing looked tempting, but she did see some bottled mineral water and helped herself to one.

Not wanting to disturb her mom's nap, she slipped back to her room to try to reach Josh again since he still hadn't responded. "Hey, Josh, r u ok?" she texted. She was suddenly worried. *What if he was in a car wreck? What if he was really sick?* She pondered what to do. She didn't know how to reach his roommate but made a mental note to get his cell next time she talked to Josh. *Maybe his phone is dead? Yeah, that's probably what happened. He'll notice it eventually and put it on the charger.*

She wanted to talk to someone, so she sent out a couple texts to a few of her friends. She sent one to Emma, who was one of the most compassionate people she had ever met. After a few texts back and forth, Emma called, and they talked for a while, and Emma was able to give her a lot of comfort. She then texted with Kendi a little bit, then sent a group text to Hope, Amanda, Lexi, and Hailey from church. They were all really supportive.

She could practically hear Amanda's southern accent as she read her text: "Y'all gonna be ok in the cold?"

Amie laughed inwardly. *It's not as if we are staying in an igloo.* But she texted, "Yes, the house is toasty warm, so no problem. I'm guessing I'll be back in a few days."

"We miss ya, girl," Hailey added to the group text.

"We'll be praying," Lexi assured her.
"Keep us posted," Hope's request read.

Amie heard her mom talking on the phone, so she went back into the living room. She heard her mom say, "Here's Amie now, I'll put you on speaker."

"Hi, Honey," Amie heard her dad's voice.

"Hi, Daddy," she answered back, wishing for all the world that he was there to hug her.

"Are you doing okay?"

"Yeah, I'm fine. I'm super sad that Grandpa died. It was so sudden. He seemed like he was just fine and then before we knew it, he was gone!"

"I know. I think we'll all be in shock for a little while. It's been a hard day for you and Mom. I wish I was with you. I'm flying out of Spokane first thing in the morning, and we'll all be together. Uncle Bob will drive me to Spokane. You guys can pick me up at the airport just before lunch. It will be good to hug my girls!"

"Well, we can't wait to see you!" Staci shared the sentiment. "In the meantime, I'll be working out some of the details. It sounds like Gail is going to come tomorrow, too. She was able to get a bereavement ticket, so it won't cost her a fortune. It will feel good to have the four of us here to figure things out together."

They finished the conversation with Randy. Amie and her mom chatted a bit, then they went to bed. When Amie woke up the next morning, she grabbed her phone and saw that Josh had responded to her text with a quick note: "Sorry, I was studying with a friend. Talk soon!"

Amie was surprised that he had written such a quick reply after all her urgent texts and her voicemail, but she figured there must be a reason.

"Call when you can," Amie texted. "It's important!"

Her mom was already busy on her computer, presumably researching all the things that needed to be handled when someone passes away. She told Amie that she and Gail would likely be here in Montana for a couple weeks getting the paperwork filed, the house packed, and the house listed on the real estate market.

In the meantime, they'd send Amie back with her dad, possibly tomorrow. They could fly to Seattle, pick up the car, and drive it back to Chelan. Amie agreed that it was a good plan, but she wanted to do as much as she could to help before they left. Staci said they would start by going to the store and getting some boxes to pack up the extensive collection of her dad's books. There were also lots of her mom's cookbooks, even though she had died over a decade ago. There would be a lot of things to go through, so they found the boxes at the store and set about packing them up.

Soon, it was time to pick up Randy at the airport, and, as luck would have it, Gail's flight came in at about the same time, so they all were able to ride home together. After a quick lunch at the diner that included four amazing slices of pie shared between the four of them, they headed to the house and spent the rest of the afternoon packing, reminiscing, and filling out essential paperwork. Gail looked just as Amy remembered. She was a tall, slim lady with shoulder-length blonde hair and blue eyes, similar to Amie and her mom. She was a marketing professional and always looked put-together, even when she was dressed comfortably, like today.

"So, no memorial service, right?" Gail asked.

"No, he didn't want one, and I feel like we need to honor his request," Staci replied. "I know that he would want any memorial gifts to go toward some sort of a scholarship fund at the college, so we can discuss that with them, and we can add it to the obituary."

"When I was on the plane, I took a stab at writing one," Gail said. "I hope I wasn't stepping on your toes."

"Not at all. I haven't even thought about it yet," Staci assured her. The two of them sat at the table and worked through the obituary while Amie and her dad did their best to sort items. They packed up the things that they knew had no sentimental value and left things that they knew Staci and Gail would have to deal with together. Amie and her dad worked as quickly as they could to lessen the giant workload the two sisters would have to deal with in the coming weeks.

They were still packing at seven in the evening when pizza arrived, sent by a neighbor who had heard what was going on. Amie and her family dug into the pizza, and it fueled them for several more hours of work.

It was determined that Randy and Amie would spend two more days in Montana, then catch a flight back to Seattle. They figured out sleeping arrangements and settled in for the night.

The next morning, after Gail and Staci had figured out the paperwork, they turned their attention to helping Amie and Randy pack up the house. Gail worked with Amie, and Staci worked with Randy. Gail and Amie had a good time laughing at some of the strange things Grandpa Peterson had accumulated through the years in all of his travels. Amie suggested that Gail could move to Chelan, so they could hang out with her more because she was so fun.

Gail laughed and responded, "If you can figure out a way to make your spectacular summers last all year long, we can talk. Otherwise, my feet are firmly planted in the sand on Maui."

"I don't blame you," Amie responded. "Year-round summer sounds pretty fantastic to me!"

As they were packing, they were all thankful that Grandpa Peterson was a minimalist, barring his extensive book collection, which proved to be easy to pack and donate.

By late Wednesday afternoon, when Gail and Staci dropped Randy and Amie off at the airport for their flight to SeaTac airport, a good chunk of the house had been packed up, and the task did not seem as insurmountable as it had a few days prior. With lots of hugs and well-wishes, Amie and her dad were on their way to their room in the resort they would call home during the next few weeks of their "reno-cation."

CHAPTER TEN

Waterville

When Amie started back to school on Thursday, one of her assignments was to research a small town in Washington State and prepare both a written report and a presentation to give the class. The students were assigned their town by a drawing. When Amie reached into the white plastic bucket, she pulled out a blue slip of paper that said Waterville. *Waterville...*Amie thought to herself. That sounds familiar. *I think it's nearby, but I don't think I've ever been there. Maybe I can drive out there and check it out in person.*

Ms. Whipple, Amie's teacher, had each student announce the name of the town they had drawn and had the other students raise their hands if they had heard of it. She listened to what the other students had selected at random and was able to raise her hand as having heard about half of them, mainly because they had been an opposing team for one of their school sports. From what Amie could tell, the cities and towns were spread all over the state. The towns had names such as Asotin, Benton City, Cashmere, Cle Elum, Colfax, Davenport, Dayton, Forks, Friday Harbor, Gold Bar, Long Beach, Medina, McCleary, Okanogan, Rainier, Royal City, Touchet, Wallula, Waterville, and Zillah. The teacher gave them two days plus the weekend to research these cities, then they would spend the next week giving oral reports complete with pictures, graphs and other visual aids. People who volunteered to present on Monday got five extra credit points on the assignment. Amie immediately raised her hand to present on Monday, as did a few other students. Miss Whipple explained that the written reports would be due at the end of next week. *Hmm…plenty of time for the written report, but not too much time to prepare for the oral presentations,* Amie thought. Miss Whipple passed out the rubric that explained the minimum that students would need to do to receive a C. It also explained what a B and an A would need to incorporate.

Amie was excited to start her research. On assignments like this, the expectations for an A grade were the minimum she would allow herself to complete, and she generally tried to raise the bar by including other creative elements. She was excited to sink her teeth into this assignment because she wanted to get her mind off the trauma she experienced with her grandpa's death on Sunday and the hands-off approach Josh was taking to her grief.

She had only spoken with Josh twice since Sunday. Once was on Monday afternoon, when he finally returned her call, and she was able to tell him about their trip to Missoula and the fact that her grandpa has passed away. He had expressed sympathy at that time but they ended up talking more about what he was doing at school. The other time they talked was when Amie was in the Missoula airport waiting for her flight back yesterday. This was a shorter conversation because Josh only had a short time in between his classes at UW. He spoke sympathetically to Amie, but it sounded like his mind was elsewhere. Amie had expected Josh to be a little more involved in what she was going through, but she understood that freshman classes were tough, and Josh had lots of homework. She was actually glad that he was not coming back this weekend because she did not want to be distracted from this project since she would need the whole weekend to prepare.

At lunchtime, Amie texted her dad and asked if she could drive to Waterville when she got out of school since it wasn't too far, and she had to do a report on it.

Amie read his reply, "How about if I go with you?"

"Awesome. Meet at the resort at 3:15?" Amie typed.

"Perfect," he texted back.

Thoughts of the upcoming trip to Waterville gave Amie the impetus to put aside the sad thoughts about her grandpa's death and Josh's busyness and focus on her schoolwork.

****

Promptly at 3:15, Amie, driving her mom's car, pulled into the resort parking lot and was greeted by her dad.

"Ready?" he asked.

"Yep!" Amie agreed, getting out of the driver's seat and hopping into the passenger side of her mom's car. Her dad got behind the wheel, and they played some Lauren Daigle music as they drove. Amie noticed that some of the trees still had not dropped their fall leaves as they gave into the chill of the upcoming winter.

Amie asked her dad, "How are mom and Gail doing?"

"They're doing great. They have had some good moments going through all their parents' things. She said they have cried, but they've also laughed a lot. Grieving is a process. It's good they can be together."

"I agree. I know they're going to be meeting with a realtor this evening, so that'll be good," Amie added.

"It's a well-maintained home, and it will show well." He then shifted gears and asked, "So why are we going to Waterville? You said it was for a class?"

"Yeah, we are each doing reports on small towns in Washington, and I drew Waterville out of a whole bucket of places. I am lucky because we live close, so we can visit it, take pictures, and hopefully talk to people there to learn interesting things about the town."

"Why don't you just do a search online?"

"Oh, Dad! I can get the facts online, but I wanted my report to be more comprehensive and include more of the flavor of the town."

"Well, you always have been an overachiever like your mom," Randy commented proudly.

"I think that if you're gonna do something, you should do it right," Amie declared. "I'm looking forward to this to keep my mind off of...everything."

"Well, I don't blame you. It must have been a terrible experience to have been with your grandpa when..." he trailed off.

"Yes, it was surreal," Amie agreed. "It still doesn't seem real, even four days later. I thought we were just going to be there to help Grandpa get better and cook for him and stuff, I never thought we would have a conversation with him and leave for a little while and then come back to, well, you know."

"Yes, it was tough on both of you, but you are only a teen. That had to be devastating," Randy sympathized.

"I know. I don't know if he is in Heaven or where he is right now," Amie commented. "When we were there earlier in the day, he didn't seem interested in discussing it, and when we returned, he was basically unresponsive. The chaplain said that we don't know what kind of decision he may have made during his final moments, and we could hold on to that hope."

"I think that's all you can do," Randy agreed. He then drove into town. "This appears to be Locust Street and Chelan Avenue," he commented as they entered Waterville.

"Chelan Avenue," Amie repeated. "That's not too creative. I wonder how they name streets?"

"I'm not sure," Randy admitted. "And how, of all the names in the world, did they choose Locust as a name in an agricultural area? Locusts can kill a harvest. I'm not sure that they deserve a street named after them."

Amie smiled as she thought through the logic in that statement. "Maybe one of the founding families had the last name of Locust, and that is where that street derives its name," Amie suggested.

"That would make more sense," Randy agreed. "So, what's your plan for discovering the 'flavor' of the town, as you put it?"

"I think we should drive around and see everything, then stop by somewhere that has some cars in the parking lot, go in, and have some meaningful conversations," Amie decided.

"Okay. You're in charge. Just tell me where you want to go," Randy responded.

Amie pulled out her phone and looked at a map of the town. "Oooohh, Locust Street is named after the *tree,* not the insect, *nor* a person. A lot of the streets here are named after trees."

"Well, this appears to be the end of town. Where should we stop?"

"Let's see if there are officials available to talk with."

Amie and her dad had some luck when a lady at the store directed them to the mayor, who was able to give them a tour and a lot of good information for Amie's report.

****

On the way home, Amie's mom called, so they listened to her together over the car's speaker system.

Staci mentioned that they had finalized the obituary and that the graphics person at the newspaper helped them to select the best photo to use from the three they had submitted. The plans for the memorial scholarship were going well, and she and Gail were happy with how the college was setting it up. Staci and Gail had managed to keep some mementos, sell a few large items of furniture on Craigslist, and donate quite a bit of stuff to places that could use it. The realtor was coming by to take photos tomorrow, and Staci believed that the place looked pretty good. The realtor advised them that the market was so hot right now, they would likely sell quickly for a good price, regardless of whether it looked perfect or not.

"You better believe that was music to our ears," Staci commented. "We are both exhausted, and we did not relish the idea of painting everything, replacing carpets, updating fixtures, and all that. We're happy to let the next owner do it. We both just want to come home!"

"Is Gail coming back with you?" Amie called out to be heard over the speaker.

"Yes, she said that she would spend a couple days with us at the resort before she heads back to Maui!"

"Yay!" Amie squealed. "It'll be fun to have her here."

"Definitely. I'll let you know when we are coming so that you can have Debbie block a room for Gail."

"Sounds good! Everything else okay?" Randy asked.

"Yes. We're about to get going and get something to eat. Oh, I forgot to tell you, we lined up a buyer for dad's car, and he said he could wait a few days until we needed to leave town."

"What about the rental car?"

"We returned it yesterday."

"Okay, well, it sounds like you guys have things well under control."

"Well, we can tell that God does, at least. Things have been going smoothly, so we know that He is taking care of stuff for us. Love you guys! Talk to you tomorrow."

"Good night, Honey," Randy replied.

"Good night, Mom!" Amie called.

They hung up and pulled into the driveway of the resort. Amie gathered her laptop and some books into a black padded Calvin Klein bag and went to the reading room of the resort to do her homework. The reading room had lots of bookshelves, a couple couches, and some tables and chairs. It also had a gas fireplace that turned on via remote control. The cozy room was a hidden gem at the resort this time of year, so Amie took full advantage of the empty space, spread out her schoolwork on the table, and got to work.

She thought about texting Josh, but she knew he was busy and would text when he could. She sighed. *This long-distance relationship thing is frustrating!* She pouted a moment, then turned her attention to the Waterville report. The gleam in her eye returned as she pulled out the rubric and organized her report to ensure it hit all the required elements plus some of the optional ones. Her slender fingers flew deftly over her keyboard and, by the time her dad texted her to find out where she was, she had already typed for two hours and had a good start on her report.

She looked at the time on her phone with surprise and texted her dad back: "I'm in the reading room and I'm getting a lot done. I still need another hour to catch up with all my classes, then I'll be back in the room."

Her dad responded, "Ok – see ya there."

Amie reluctantly closed her laptop and opened up her more mundane homework. Her trig class was starting to get hard, and she knew she had to buckle down and catch up with what she missed when she was gone, or nothing else going forward would make sense in that class. Luckily, after about a half hour, she decided that she had the hang of the current unit and finished her assignments. She then moved onto her Spanish homework and was glad to see that the current lesson incorporated a lot of review words.

After Spanish, she opened her physics book and thought of the last conversation she had with her grandpa, and her eyes filled with tears. *I never got to talk with him about physics. He would have been able to explain all this stuff to me and would have enjoyed doing it. How is it fair that I lost him just when I finally was taking the subject that he had taught his whole career?*

Amie was alone in the warm room, and she grabbed a box of tissues and had a full-on cry session, the first major one she had since her grandpa died. When she was finished, her head ached, her eyes burned, and she felt worn out. She did not want to do any homework and was tempted to put it all away, but she pushed through and completed her physics homework. She felt a sense of relief that she had that assignment behind her.

She really wanted someone to talk to right now, and she wanted it to be Josh. She looked at her phone. *Ten o'clock now. Not too late.*

She texted him: "Can we talk?"

He texted back: "I guess so."

Amie frowned and thought to herself: *Josh definitely has seemed different lately. Maybe he is tired. I really need him, though.*

She answered on the opening note of her ring tone.

"Hi, Josh," she began.

"Hey, Amie," he answered. "What's up?" He sounded nice. Maybe she was wrong to feel irritated with him.

"Nothing. I was just sad and wanted to hear your voice."

"Oh, what are you sad about?" Josh asked.

"My grandpa," Amie responded, surprised that he asked.

"Oh yeah, I forgot that he passed," Josh said.

Amie just sat in stunned silence for a moment. *How in the world could he forget that this just happened to me? It's a BIG deal.* "You seriously forgot?" she asked, trying for all the world to manufacture a scenario where it would be excusable that he forgot about her grandpa passing away that week.

"Oh. No. Of course I didn't forget. I meant that I didn't know if that was what you were sad about, or if it was something else. Like another thing might have happened. I didn't know. Of course, you are sad about your grandpa, that makes sense," Josh stammered.

Amie decided to accept his explanation because, with her whole heart, she wanted it to be true.

So," she began, "I was sitting here doing my physics homework and then I remembered that my grandpa was a physics teacher, and we never had a single conversation about physics, and now he is gone, and I will never be able to have that conversation..."

"Oh. Yeah. Um...I'm so sorry, Amie, but my other line is ringing, and I need to take it. Could you hold on just a sec?"

"Sur..." he cut to the other line before she even got the word fully pronounced.

A full four minutes later, he came back to Amie's call. In the meantime, she had gathered up her stuff, put the phone on speaker, and began walking back to the resort room where she and her dad were staying. She had almost forgotten that she was on the line with him when she heard his voice. "Okay, sorry, Amie. What were you saying?"

"Who was that?" Amie demanded.

"Oh, it is someone who is in one of my group projects. She just needed some clarification. Back to you. Are you still sad about your grandpa and the chemistry class?"

"Physics, Josh! NOT chemistry. He was a physics teacher, and I am taking physics right now, not chemistry," Amie explained wearily. "Josh, I'm really tired, so I'm gonna go to sleep now. We can talk some other time."

"Sure. I hope you feel better, Amie."

"Thanks, Josh. Have a good night."

"Night, Amie," he murmured.

Amie hung up her phone and set it in her black bag. By now, she had reached her room. She sat her books down, took her pajamas into the bathroom, and got ready for bed. She was asleep before her dad came back to the room, but her pillow was damp from her silent tears. She slept soundly until her phone alarm woke her at six the next morning.

CHAPTER ELEVEN

Semi Finals

Amie's world was slowly returning back to normal. Her mom had returned to Chelan with Aunty Gail, and they had a lot of fun laughing reminiscing about Amie's grandpa and scheming about the next time they could get together with Aunty Gail. All the fun with Aunt Gail distracted Amie a bit from her confusion about Josh's behavior.

"I think we should visit you in Maui," Amie declared.

"I think so, too! We'll have to make that happen," Gail agreed.

Time with Aunty Gail came to an end too soon, and the next day, Randy and Staci took her to the airport to catch her flight back to Kahului.

****

Soon, it was time for Amie to give her report on Waterville, and she was prepared.

179

She showed a slideshow with historical photos she found online, along with current photos that she took when she visited. She reported on the history of the dryland wheat-farming town and included tidbits she learned from personally interviewing a knowledgeable police officer, the mayor, and a couple long-term residents. She discussed Waterville's location and showed it on a map, discussing how the town's topography was flat and boasted breathtaking views during the different seasons of the year. She mentioned that Waterville held the distinction of being situated at the highest elevation of all incorporated towns in Washington at 2800 feet. Amie brought up the ever-popular North Central Washington Fair and Rodeo that took place in Waterville the last week of August every year. She closed with a video of herself and the mayor walking through the streets of Waterville as they discussed the town. Even though the footage was shot by her dad on her phone and was edited by Amie on her laptop, it looked professional. By the time her time ran out, everyone agreed with the teacher that Amie had set the bar pretty high for the city presentations.

That night, Amie put the finishing touches on the written city report and was glad to put that assignment behind her, so she could focus on her other classes.

****

There was a lot of excitement in the air. Chelan's girls' soccer team had made it all the way to the state championship game and had narrowly missed being the state champions. Amie's friend Hope and her teammates, many of whom were seniors, were bitterly disappointed, but were happy to have made it that far. Hope was a junior this year and set her sights on redemption for the team next year.

At the same time that the girls were playing in the state championship game in Western Washington, the football team was winning their quarter finals game across the state. The semi-final game was to be played the following Saturday afternoon in Spokane.

Josh had come back to town to spend Thanksgiving with his parents, and Amie had been nervous to see him. It had been several weeks since he had been back, and their phone conversations had lacked the easy rapport that they had shared last summer and earlier in the fall. Amie hoped that when they saw each other, they would pick up right where they left off. Josh had assured her that he missed her and was looking forward to seeing her and going to the football game.

Josh was scheduled to arrive home on Wednesday afternoon, and Amie gave him space so he could see his family first. However, he hadn't texted her yet, so, around 8:30 that night, she went to the store, and she intentionally drove by his house to make sure his car was there and that he'd made it home. It was parked in front of the house with a layer of frost on it, so Amie knew it had been parked there for at least a few hours.

The next day was Thanksgiving, and they enjoyed the meal with her Aunt Debbie, Uncle Bob, and Amie's cousin George. The day came and went, and at around eight o'clock on Thanksgiving night, she received her first text from Josh since he had arrived home.

"Hey Amie, sorry I've been so busy since I've been home! I'll c ya tmrw in Spokane," he texted.

Amie had salty tears in her eyes when she read the text. She was tired of giving him the benefit of the doubt. She spent the rest of the evening trying to figure out what to say to him when she saw him and how to respond to his text now.

She responded to his text with a simple, "Okay."

****

The next day was Black Friday. That fact was not lost on Amie and her mom. They had planned to go to Spokane really early on Friday morning and hit the malls before they checked into the hotel that afternoon. Amie's dad was catching a ride up to the hotel after work with his brother Bob, his wife Debbie, and George.

On the way to Chelan, Amie confided in her mom about how Josh had been acting lately. Staci tried to remain neutral about the situation and agreed that it was good that they would have a chance to see each other face to face and talk. Amie and her mom had a good time shopping the sales, despite Amie's sadness about her relationship with Josh. *Retail therapy is definitely a thing*, Amie observed. Both Amie and her mom bought new winter coats and a couple sweaters that were on crazy-low prices. Amie got a pair of high-heeled black boots that would take her winter fashion game to the next level, but they would not be particularly helpful for walking in the snow, as her mom pointed out.

The Chelan contingency showed up in force on Friday afternoon. They basically took over one of the large Spokane hotels with the team, their families, and all their fans. Everywhere was a sea of green and gray school colors, and Amie pitied the poor person who unwittingly booked a room in this hotel for a quiet weekend. The air was loud and electric, and there were groups spread out all over the lobby with snacks. Amie and a couple of her friends went from group to group chatting excitedly and sampling the treats. It was sort of like an indoor tailgate party the evening before the game.

Amie looked up at one point, and right in front of her, entering the lobby from the parking lot, dressed in a pea coat with a classy winter scarf, was Josh. Amie's heart skipped a beat when she saw him. He looked like he just stepped out of a winter photo shoot for a designer fragrance ad. He gave her a big hug, took her hand, and led her over to a corner of the lobby to talk.

"Hey, girl, it's good to see you." He shot her a grin that almost made her forgive his inattentiveness. Almost. *He would have to do a little better than that,* she decided.

"So, you've been busy," Amie said, trying hard to maintain a hands-off approach when all she wanted to do is reconcile and forget about how he had been treating her.

"Oh, yeah, school has been really busy."

"Have you had any fun?" Amie asked.

"Not much. Sometimes, when we are in our study group, we all need a break, so we do something else. But mostly we study whenever we are not in class."

"Wow, that doesn't sound fun. UW must be hard."

"Yeah, it is," Josh maintained. "But enough about me. How is everything going with you?"

"It's been a little crazy living at the resort. Our renovations are going to be over soon, and we can get back into the house. We are all looking forward to that. I just finished doing a report on Waterville..." Amie was interrupted when some of his friends who graduated with him last year spotted him and shoved him around in a manly greeting. He chatted with his friends for a little while until they moved on. Josh turned his attention back to Amie.

"Sorry, Amie, what were you saying?"

"Nothing," she sighed inwardly. This was not the loving reconciliation she had hoped for. "Josh, I guess I want to know if you want to just be friends? It seems like you might be too busy for a relationship right now."

Josh seemed taken aback. "Is that what *you* want?" he asked. "I still like you. I think you are the cutest girl in Chelan, and I am lucky to have you," he continued.

Amie blushed under the compliments, and she courageously replied, "My feelings haven't changed, but I think I have been getting a little resentful because you don't have any time for me. Like when my grandpa died; I really needed support, and you didn't have time for me."

"Yeah, I can see that. I'm sorry about that, Amie. I'll do better about being there for you. We can work on it together and try to figure out this long-distance thing."

"Okay," she replied, giving in and forgiving him.

They talked for quite a while, warmed by the glow of the hotel fireplace. After a while, Amie looked at her phone and realized it was almost 11, and her parents had requested that she be back in the room by then. She told Josh that she needed to get upstairs, but she would see him tomorrow.

They walked to the elevator. "Give me a hug," he asked. She leaned into his arms.

Hmmm…he smells like he is in a fragrance ad, too. He thinks he is lucky, but I think I am the fortunate one, she thought to herself and went to bed that night happier than she had been in several weeks.

****

The next day, the crowd filled the outdoor stadium for the game, and it was a cold one. Amie was excited to show off the new outfit she bought yesterday, but it soon became evident that she would need to remain huddled under a blanket the whole time to keep warm.

Her friends Amanda, Lexi, and Hailey had driven up from Chelan the morning of the game, and they brought a couple blankets with them. The four girls clustered together. Amie saw Josh hanging out with some of the guys who had graduated with him last year. He seemed so different now from summer. He seemed taller, older, and more confident. He looked like a man. Amie had never thought their two-year age difference would be a problem until now. She wondered if he would even look for her and want to sit by her. Things had gone so well last night, and she didn't want to ruin her mood with speculations. She decided to focus on cheering for the football team and enjoying time with her friends and let Josh do his thing.

The game was exciting. It was hard to believe that some of the key players, like Ben and Ryan, had just started playing football this year. Amie wondered how good they would be if they had played football in middle school and the other years of high school. They were having a tough game today against an opponent whom Amie was not familiar with. The opposing team had orange and black school colors, which Amie thought was an unfortunate choice since there are not a lot of cute orange clothes available for the students to wear for spirit days. *They would likely be stuck with just the school logo clothes. It would look like Halloween all the time,* she mused.

At half time, when Amie and her friends shuffled together, still huddled in their blankets, to get concessions, the teams were tied seven-seven. As the girls stood waiting to get to the front of the line to order their hot chocolate and nachos, Amie scanned the crowds for a glimpse at Josh. She was rewarded for her efforts and saw him talking to a few of the girls who had graduated with him last year. She knew that one of them was attending WSU, and the other one was in cosmetology school in Wenatchee. *Both of them look quite enamored with whatever Josh was saying,* Amie thought grimly. *Maybe Josh has moved on and is no longer interested in a high school girl.*

Once again, Amie steeled her resolve to enjoy her day with her friends and cheer the Chelan football team on to State. Amie removed the blanket that she was huddled under, obstinately so she could better carry her food and drink, but really so that Josh might see her in her cute new outfit. She carried her items to her seat and decided to boldly go over to Josh and talk with him. She walked up to where he was chatting with the two girls.

When he saw Amie, his eyes lit up, "Hi, Amie! I was wondering where you were!" He turned back to the other two girls and said, "Great to see you, Melanie and Kylie!"

"Bye, Josh," they chorused in artificially high voices.

He turned back to Amie. "Where are you sitting?"

Amie indicated behind her to where Hailey, Amanda, and Lexi were trying not to stare at them. "Would you like to join us?" she asked.

"Sure," Josh replied and took her hand that was covered in black leather glove and walked with her to her seat. He sat down next to her. The snow was coming down lightly, and Josh draped Amie's blanket over the two of them and kept his arm around her shoulders. She leaned against him and asked if he wanted to share the hot cocoa. He took a sip and let her have the rest. They chatted as the game started back up.

The second half was exciting from the get-go. Practically every play resulted in positive yardage, and both offenses were firing on all cylinders. With the score tied at 14, Chelan scored another touchdown, and the crowd went wild! Josh caught Amie's eye, and they high fived with each other and with Amie's other friends. Unfortunately, their kicker's foot slipped in the snow, and he missed on his point after attempt. Down by six, the orange team scored on their next possession, and they were back to a tied game. With the field getting more and more slippery, Chelan's opponent attempted a two-point conversion to pull ahead and was stopped before they reached the end zone, so the score remained tied at twenty all, ending the quarter.

Nobody was feeling cold anymore because the crowd was lit! Most people were on their feet, bringing the noise and totally investing themselves in the outcome of the game. This was Chelan's chance to go to the state tournament in the Tacoma dome next weekend, and that fact was not lost on anybody. Chelan had a much bigger cheering section than their opponent, and the difference in noise levels was significant. Amie was on cloud nine standing next to her handsome boyfriend and some of her good friends as they were cheering on their football team on to state. The evergreen trees surrounding the stadium were dusted with the gently falling snow, which created a beautiful backdrop for a green football field that was rapidly turning white.

Both teams struggled to move the ball for most of the fourth quarter. With just over three minutes to go,

Quarterback Ben Brandon threw a ten-yard pass to Ryan, who deftly dodged the defenders from the orange team and looked like he was close to scoring a touchdown when he was taken down at the ten-yard line. The next play was a run play by Ben that was stopped with a tackle after just two yards. Amie never knew how to cheer on these types of plays because, yes, he was stopped, but he did get positive yardage, so, celebrate the win, right? She always took her cues from the crowd around her since she didn't understand all the nuances of football.

On the third down, Ben threw a pass to Ryan, which he caught in the endzone with two minutes left in the game, and the crowd went *wild!* Josh picked Amie up and swung her around, and all the fans were waving whatever green and gray paraphernalia that they had brought to cheer the team on. They ran a risky two-point conversion and were successful, all but cementing their victory.

The orange team got the ball after that and had a couple long runs before they were stopped by Chelan. The game down to a fourth down with 18 seconds to play and the ball on the 45-yard line. Everyone knew that their only path to victory was a big play, and almost nobody expected it to happen. Their talented quarterback received the ball from the center and, despite a valiant effort from Chelan's defense, managed to throw a perfect spiral down the field to one of his receivers who darted it over the line into the endzone for a score. Chelan's team was livid, and the opponent's fans were going crazy from the unexpected turn of events. Amie was convinced the noise from the stands was loud enough to shatter eardrums. With a mere ten seconds left in the game, the opposing team had to score on a two-point conversion to tie the game and send it into overtime.

Fortunately, their conversion attempt was thwarted by Chelan's defense, and their onside kick attempt was recovered by Chelan. The football team was headed to the state tournament for the first time in recent history. The excitement in the air Amie felt earlier paled compared with the excitement going on now.

The crowd and players were frozen from the snowy weather, but their spirits were on fire. Perfect strangers were hugging each other, screaming, fist-bumping, and high-fiving. Josh grabbed Amie's hand and drug her down the concrete steps to where some of the alumni from his class were celebrating. Amie got her share of high-fives there as well, and Josh and the other guys discussed the game in excited tones. Amie was proud to be by Josh's side as he hung out with his friends.

As the crowd finally began to dissipate, he asked Amie if she would want to go out to dinner with him before she headed back to the hotel. She looked for her parents, who she knew were sitting close to the front on the left side during the game, because she wanted to ask their permission first. They were clustered with Amie's aunt and uncle and some other friends up by the concession stand, where it looked like they just got refills on coffee. Amie told Josh she would ask her parents. She hustled back up the concrete steps to where her mom was standing.

"Is it okay if I go to dinner with Josh before we come back to the hotel?" Amie asked.

"Sure!" her mom replied, then, catching Amie's eye, asked, "Are things going better?"

"Yes!" Amie said, her eyes shining. "What a game!"

"Definitely," her mom agreed. "I'm glad we came!"

"We're going to Tacoma next weekend, right?" Amie confirmed.

"Dad and I'll figure it out tonight," Staci promised.

"Okay, well, see you guys later tonight!" Amie replied and ran down to meet Josh. On the way down, she saw Amanda, who told her that she and Lexi and Hailey were on the way home, but they couldn't wait until next weekend in Tacoma.

"Absolutely! We are spending the night at the hotel tonight, so I won't see you at church, but I will see you at Bible study tomorrow night. Have a safe trip home!" Amie called after her.

By now, Josh had joined her near the top of the stairs. "Ready to go, Sandy?"

"Sandy?" Amie asked angrily.

"Yeah, remember when we went to the drive-in this summer, and you looked like Sandy from Grease?"

"Oh, sorry, I missed the reference," Amie explained.

"Okay, *Amie*," Josh emphasized, "Let's go get some dinner!" He took her hand and walked her to his car, opened the passenger door for her, and closed it.

Finding a restaurant that wasn't totally packed was a trick, but they were able to get a table at a pizza joint with only a twenty-minute wait. They sat down and ordered a combo pizza. They enjoyed their slices, but they weren't able to have a successful conversation due to all the noise around them. Josh suggested that they go to ice cream afterwards, where they could talk.

They found an ice cream parlor, and ordered a banana split. Josh apologized again for being so busy and not being there for her when her grandpa died. He promised to be better at responding to her texts and calls.

"Am I forgiven?" Josh asked, smiling expectantly.

"Of course," Amie answered. "I guess I'm more high-maintenance than I thought."

"No, your grandpa passing away unexpectedly was a huge deal, and I should have been there for you. I'll do better," he resolved.

"Okay. Let's put that to rest, and you can fill me in on U-dub," Amie suggested.

"Sounds good. Well, it's huge," he began. "There are tons of dorms, and the campus is spacious. My dorm is small. My roommate is super studious, and he is always studying on campus, so I rarely see him."

"Is he a Christian?" Amie asked.

"I don't think so. I don't think many people are, based on class talks," Josh said. "I'm not in Kansas anymore."

"Have you tried finding some Christian groups to join? What about a church?"

"No, I have been really busy. I haven't found anything that fits my schedule yet," Josh retorted.

Amie, sensing that she should back off, remarked, "Well, maybe after the holidays, you'll find something when everything starts up again."

"Yeah, maybe," Josh brightened.

"Are you going to work at the resort over the break?"

"Yeah, I will for sure. They already asked when they could put me on the schedule. It will be good to get some hours in during the busy holiday catering season."

"Good," Amie smiled. "I think they're going to put me on catering jobs, so we'll get to work together again."

"Awesome!" Josh agreed. "Should we head back to the hotel and see if everyone is still celebrating in the lobby?"

"Sounds good!" Amie replied cheerfully. Josh held her hand on the way to the car again and even when they were at red lights on the way back to the hotel.

When they got to the lobby, Josh saw some of his friends, then turned to Amie and said, "Hey, Amie, it was fun to hang out with you. I think I am going to go catch up with some friends."

Amie was confused for a brief moment, then realized that the date was over, and he was basically dismissing her. She felt a twang of pain. *Why couldn't he bring me with him when he caught up with friends? Is he ashamed to be dating a junior?* She then quickly corrected herself and decided that it wasn't anything against her, he just wanted to hang out with the guys and talk football. *It's not like he is hanging out with other girls. I need to get over this possessive girlfriend thing. It's not very attractive.*

She looked around to see if any of her friends were around and didn't see any at the moment. She walked over to a table where her mom, dad, aunt, and uncle were playing a board game that she liked. Her mom told her to pull up a chair and help her strategize. Amie really didn't want to hang out with a bunch of adults, but that seemed to be the best option, so she sat down and partnered with her mom.

About an hour later, they finished the game, and Amie and her parents went up to their room for the night. Amie peeked over to where Josh and his friends had been hanging out and noticed that they had all left. She shrugged, tried to tell herself it was no big deal, and followed her parents to the elevator.

CHAPTER TWELVE

Road to State

The teachers at Chelan High were having a hard time keeping their students focused this week because of the excitement surrounding the football team going to State this weekend. In truth, the teachers themselves were as excited as the students were.

The football players were enjoying their moment in the sun. They walked around like celebrities and were treated as such. The cheerleaders prepared elaborate locker decorations for them, and they had lots of people help create goodie bags to send with each player.

The team bus left Chelan on Thursday after school, and cars filled the school parking lot and the surrounding street as people lined up for the send-off. Mr. Hawk, the athletic director, had rooms for the players at a small hotel near the stadium, but he reserved a room block with a discount rate for families and fans in a larger hotel, which had a big lobby for the after-game celebration. In truth, he wanted the players to be sequestered away from their excited parents and other students. He did not want them distracted or pestered by family members, girlfriends, and classmates. He promised that they would have a big celebration for the team, win or lose.

Amie's parents had booked a suite at the hotel for the girls in her Bible Study group, and they divided the price among the seven girls who would be attending. A couple sets of their parents were going, so they divided the girls between the cars. Amie's aunt and uncle drove their large SUV, and Amie, Hope, and Lexi shared the back seat. Amie was happy to have some time to catch up with Hope and hear about her soccer season.

While they were in the van, Amie remembered that a rumor had been going around the school that several of the girls had gone out drinking the night before their championship game, and their hangovers may have led to the loss. Amie gingerly asked Hope about it.

"So, the soccer team had a great season," Amie began. "Second in state is awesome!"

"Yeah," Hope agreed with a shrug. "It is cool that we went that far, but it's lame that we lost the final game."

"Any truth to the rumor that the players were hung over?" Lexi blurt out, shattering the groundwork that Amie was carefully putting in place.

"I can't comment on that," Hope replied evenly. "I can tell you that I personally did not see any alcohol when we were there, nor was I invited to any place where there may have been some. But I don't know for sure if anything happened or not."

Hope's comment was enough to show that she didn't want the speculation to continue, so Amie steered the conversation in another direction: "So, Hope, are you still enjoying Chelan?"

"I really am. The trees in the fall were so beautiful, and the snow on the crests of the hills is really pretty, too."

"Have you moved out of The Guesthouse yet?" Lexie asked.

"Yes! My mom and I moved into my uncle's house last weekend, and it is great," she grinned. "We are going to plant a garden in the spring."

"Has basketball season started?" Amie inquired.

"It has. I'm not really into it, though. I think I'd rather just work at my uncle's store. But I'm committed to the team this year. I'll see how it goes. Maybe next year, I'll do something different."

"Yeah, sports take up a lot of time," Lexi commented. "I play tennis, and I feel like I have no time in the spring."

"I know. I used to not care because my life was different in Lynnwood, but here, I want to work harder on my school work, and it is fun to work at Everything Outdoors with my mom. She is so excited to run the store with my Uncle Joe!"

"Maybe you could take the spring sports season off?" Amie suggested hopefully. "You are normally on the track team, right?"

"Yes, I'm thinking about that. We'll see," Hope answered. "What's going on with you, Lexi?"

"I have been busy teaching piano lessons after school. I have five students right now," Lexi shared, "and I go into Wenatchee every Saturday to work with a private tennis coach, so I'm keeping occupied," she laughed.

"I guess so," Amie agreed. "Do you think you might get a scholarship for tennis or for music?"

"I'm going to apply for both. My mom is pretty obsessive, and she has been researching scholarships since last year, when my brother went through the process. I'll do like he did and let my mom do the research, then I'll write an essay whenever my mom tells me to for whatever scholarship she finds," Lexi sighed.

Hope looked worried. "Yikes. I didn't know it was that complicated."

"I think for just athletics, it might not be that bad. You have to have a highlight reel to send to the schools you are interested in, but your coach or Mr. Hawk can help with that," Lexi speculated while Amie nodded encouragingly, hoping Lexi was correct.

"What do you mean by 'Mr. Hawk?'" Hope mentioned with suspicion. She was hoping nobody knew that her mom and Mr. Hawk had developed a friendship.

"He is the athletic director. He helps the athletes when they want to apply for athletic scholarships," Lexi explained. Once again, Amie nodded as she heard this information, since she hadn't been aware of how it worked, either.

"Oh, yeah, that makes sense," Hope commented, chastising herself for drawing the wrong conclusion.

Amie's aunt Debbie called back, "Hey, everyone, we are almost to Leavenworth. We can use the restroom, grab food, or shop a *little bit* ... I'm looking at you, Amie! We'll meet back at the car in 40 minutes from now. Set your phone alarm, girls! After this stop, we are going to drive straight to Tacoma, if at all possible."

"Sounds good!" the girls called back in unison.

"Will we get to see the tree lighting?" Amie asked loud enough that her aunt would hear over all the rustling in the car.

"Yes, that will signal that it is time to get to the car," Debbie responded. Everyone was excited about that because it would be crazy not to stop for the legendry tree lighting ceremony, when they were already there at just the right time.

When the car stopped, the girls got out and made a beeline to the chocolatier. There was a vendor selling roasted chestnuts that Lexi had wanted to try because of the reference in the Christmas song. Lexi bought a small bag, tasted them, and declared them to be "mushy." Hope and Amie also tried them and were similarly disappointed.

The fragrance of the different food offerings mingling together was tantalizing. They bought some colorful, flavored popcorn from another vendor and were pleased with the yummy taste. The girls gobbled it hungrily, so Amie suggested they find something for dinner.

There was a food truck selling bratwursts and burgers smothered in grilled onions, so the girls each ordered food there. They shivered in the cold weather as they waited for their meal and tried to strategize about how to spend their little time in this cute town before they had to leave. They grabbed their orders when they were ready and devoured them quickly, so they could have ten minutes to shop before the tree lighting.

They darted down the main street, power shopping instead of the casual browsing they had done in past trips. Despite all the cute things to buy, all of the girls passed on the temptation to purchase anything here because they wanted to save their money in case they needed it for the rest of the trip. They made it out of the shops just as the trees were lighting up, and they got to observe the full effect of this Bavarian wonderland in all its winter glory.

Hope announced, "It is so beautiful, but we need to get to the car right away!" The other girls agreed, and they hustled to the parking area and got in and buckled before most of the rest of the group arrived.

"Okay, looks like we're all aboard to Tacoma!" Debbie announced happily as they vacated the parking lot and entered a stream of traffic heading down the mountain highway. The girls had blankets in the backseat and curled up the best they could to nap on the way to Tacoma. The lights in Seattle woke Amie up, and it took a minute for her to figure out where she was and what she was doing. Then, she realized that tomorrow was the State football championship. Lexi and Hope soon woke up as well, and they jumped into some more lively conversations. Hope asked Amie if Josh was coming to the game.

"Oh, yes, he wouldn't miss it. He is friends with most of the players," she added.

"Will Conner be there?" Lexi asked Hope.

"Yes! He took the bus to Seattle. He is staying with Brett at his dorm, and they are going to drive over for the game."

"How are things going with him?" Lexi asked.

"We are taking it slowly," Hope replied with finality that conveyed that she didn't want to continue this line of questioning.

Amie told them the story of her and her mom's Black Friday shopping adventures, how she was finally able to find the perfect black winter boots for the season, *and* the fact that they were on sale. "I'm going to wear them for the game tomorrow. These boots I am wearing now are flat and cozy, but I want a different look for the stadium."

They then felt the car slowing down as it approached a freeway exit.

"Are we there?" Amie asked excitedly.

"Yep, this is our exit," her uncle called back. They drove around a little bit and found their hotel, and Amie's uncle Bob pulled into the check-in lane. Staci got everyone checked in, Amie's dad Randy grabbed a luggage cart, and Bob popped the hatch so they could load up the luggage. By the time they got the bags and Bob parked, the ladies had the room keys doled out.

"Amie, the other girls in the room can pick up their keys from the front desk when they arrive. You can text them and let them know that they will need to show their identification," her mom instructed.

"Okay," Amie said with a nod as she quickly typed a message into her phone to the other girls, Bailey, Hailey, Amanda, and Sunni. "They are about a half hour away," she reported to Hope and Lexi.

The lobby of the hotel was spacious and beautifully appointed with lush carpeting and crystal chandeliers. Once again, it seemed that the hotel was nearly empty except for the Chelan fans. Amie's dad explained that since this type of hotel was used a lot by business travelers, Friday nights were often a slow time for them. The common area of the hotel had lots of tables, chairs, and couches spread out, and, once again, the tailgate-type atmosphere ruled the evening. There were more families and alumni who showed up this week than last since this weekend was the actual state championship game, and people who bought their ticket would be able to watch the other divisions' championship games as well as Chelan's, so it would be an exciting day of football.

Like last time, the girls made their rounds and were able to see former Chelan students who were now in college and had come to Tacoma for the game. Amie knew that she wouldn't see Josh until tomorrow when he drove up from his dorm to attend the games. She enjoyed walking around with her girlfriends, mingling with various groups of people. She and her mom had come prepared with treats they had made this week. Staci also made an enormous amount of Chex mix, which she made available to everyone.

By midnight, most people had headed up to their rooms, and Amie and her friends decided to do the same. Someone had mentioned that the indoor pool stayed open all night, and they confirmed that rumor with the front desk staff. The girls went to their suite, put on swimsuits and coverups, and padded down the hall to the elevator, trying to stay quiet, but giggling all the same.

They rode the elevator down to the pool and were glad to see it was empty. The girls did some jumping and diving contests and laughingly choreographed a synchronized swimming routine. They were loud, but the pool was a distance away from any of the guest rooms, so they didn't disturb anyone. After they were cold from the pool, they settled down and sat in the hot tub together.

They started to play truth or dare and ask each other silly questions, like who their favorite player was on the football team or which one of their teachers was most likely to have a secret life. Lexi selected dare, and Amanda dared her to swim to the center of the pool, take off her swimsuit while she was under water, and put it on again. Lexi shrugged and dove in the deep end, swam to the middle, and pulled the straps down on her one-piece suit and wiggled out of it. She held one hand out of the water with the suit to prove that she had done the dare.

About that time, Amie saw a couple attractive boys from another school come open the door to the pool area. She had to think quickly to avoid having them see Lexi. Hope had seen the boys enter the area as well, and, without even discussing it, she grabbed Amie's arm, and the two of them leaped out of the hot tub and intercepted the two boys and did their best to distract them, so Lexi could put her suit back on in the pool without being noticed. Hope and Amie jumped in front of the two boys and caught them by surprise.

"I'm Hope, and this is Amie. We are from Chelan," Hope announced to the two boys.

"Where are you guys from?" Amie added quickly.

"We're from Mukilteo," one of the boys answered, confused by the overly friendly girls.

"Are you here for the football tournament?" Hope asked loudly, continuing to block their view to the pool.

"Um, yeah, his dad is the coach of Bellevue Christian, and they are in the tournament, so we're here to watch the game." The boys still looked suspicious about what Amie and Hope were doing.

Out of the corner of her eye, Hope saw Lexi exit the pool, grab a towel, and wrap up in it. Hope realized that they had successfully completed her mission. She looked at Amie and said, "Let's leave these two guys alone and get out of here."

Amie looked back at her, unaware that Lexi had already exited the pool, and remarked, "But I want to hear all about Mukilteo."

"I think we're ready to go now, *all* of us, and let these guys swim."

"Ohhhhh," Amie expressed, finally understanding. "Well, it was nice to meet you guys. Have fun!"

She looked back toward the other girls and announced, "Let's go back to our room."

The other girls gathered their stuff and, wrapped up in their towels and coverups, made their way over to the door. Amie and Hope grabbed their stuff and did the same.

"Hey, you girls don't have to go on our account," one of the boys began.

"Oh, I think we do," Amie responded. "Maybe we'll see you tomorrow."

"We'll look for you at breakfast," one of the guys promised.

The seven girls scooted out of the pool area and the door barely shut behind them before they burst into peals of laughter. Amanda had a lot of apologizing to do to Lexi, and Lexi thanked Hope and Amie for their quick thinking to distract the boys.

When the girls got settled in the room where they were going to sleep, they would just start to get quiet, and someone would burst out with a comment such as, "Where is Mukilteo, anyway?" and that would set everyone off laughing again. Finally, at about two a.m., all seven girls were sound asleep, where they remained until seven in the morning.

CHAPTER THIRTEEN

Championship Game

The girls got up at various times the next morning and managed to all get showers and breakfast from the lobby in some form.

They loaded into the two cars at the appointed time. This go around, the girls in Amie's uncle's SUV were Amanda and Hailey, while Lexi and Hope rode with Bailey and Sunni. The seven girls had a great time checking out the booths that lined the Tacoma dome. There were trinkets and mementos for purchase, and sports camps and colleges were promoting their offerings. The girls filled bags with candy, giveaway pens, and notepads that were being handed out. Some of the booths had games like Plinko and a wheel to spin to get small prizes. It was like being at the fair, but these games didn't cost anything to play, and it was a great way to pass the time before their game started. One of the other divisions had their game first, so the corridor crowds dissipated as people found seats for the game.

Amie and her friends sat down, and Amie watched her phone anxiously for word that Josh had arrived. She had texted him earlier, but he had not responded, so she assumed that he was driving.

By the time the game that they were watching reached halftime, Amie decided to text Josh again. "Hey, just wondering how far out you are?" she texted. Again, she received no response, and she suppressed her urge to worry that he must have gotten in a car wreck because it wasn't unusual for him to not answer her texts for a while.

The game they were watching went into overtime and was really exciting. Amie and Hope were sitting next to each other and remarked that they were glad that they didn't have a dog in this fight, or they would be stressed about the outcome. It was nice to relax and just enjoy the game without being anxious about every play.

After that game was over, it was time for Chelan's game. They were playing Lynden Christian for the state title. The teams were already on the field conducting their pre-game warm-ups when Amie saw Josh entering Chelan's seating area with Brett and Conner. The boys came over to where Hope and Amie were seating and found seats behind them. Josh leaned forward and put his hands on Amie's shoulders, giving her a little neck and shoulder massage.

When he finished rubbing her shoulders, she turned around and said, "I was wondering if you were going to make it?"

He replied, "Yeah, we had a late night last night, so I slept in. I caught a ride up here with Brett, and it turns out that Conner was staying with him, so we all hung out last night."

"Oh, good!" Amie replied.

The teams lined up for the National Anthem, then the game began.

Every moment was exciting. Both teams were stronger on offense than defense, so they each were able to score twice before the first quarter ended. In the second quarter, each team scored a touchdown, but Chelan missed their extra point, so the score was 21-20, with Lynden Christian ahead at the half. The Chelan fans were a little dejected at half time, but still optimistic that they could get the upper hand.

When the Chelan team ran out of the locker room onto the field after half-time, they looked strong, confident, and purposeful. They completed some warmup passes and runs and looked like they were ready to fight.

The other team kicked off to them, and a Chelan player caught the ball at the twenty-yard line and, after an exciting zig zagging run, was tackled at the forty-yard line. The fans went crazy with their support. Chelan methodically moved the ball down the field, achieving first downs with each play. They got within ten yards of the goal, and Quarterback Ben Brandon got the ball. Both of his receivers had heavy coverage, so he ran it himself and dove over the goal line for six points. The crowd literally went wild after the show of athleticism. Their kicker scored the extra point easily, and now, they were six points ahead of the Lynden team. Chelan scored seven more unanswered points, the score raised to 34-21 at the end of the third quarter, and it seemed like they would be unbeatable. The Chelan fans were loud and enthusiastic. Lynden's fans looked fairly dejected, but they still tried to encourage their players.

In the fourth quarter, the momentum shifted hard, and Lynden Christian scored seven points to bring the score to a much closer 34-28, with Chelan maintaining the lead. Halfway through the quarter, Lynden Christian scored again, and both teams' fans were loud and attentive. Amie was relieved when their kick was blocked, and the point after was no good, resulting in a tie score of 34 all. If neither team scored, they would have to play in overtime, which neither of the exhausted teams wanted.

With just over four minutes to play, Lynden Christian surprisingly tried for an onside kick. Just after the ball traveled ten yards, multiple players from both teams dove for the ball, resulting in a huge pile. As the referees pulled players off the pile, the Tacoma dome got eerily quiet as both sets of fans waited anxiously to see who had the ball on the bottom of the pile. After what seemed like an eternity, the referee finally signaled that it was Chelan's ball and Amie and the other Chelan fans went wild, screaming, high-fiving, and hugging each other.

Starting with the ball near the middle of the field, Chelan made two first downs in a row, running the ball before being stuffed on their next two run plays. On third and long, Ben threw a pass that resulted in a 15-yard gain, and Chelan was now just nine yards from the end zone. The next two run plays resulted in short gains, and with just ten seconds to go, Chelan's coach called time out. Amie could hear the boys behind her speculating about what the coach must be planning.

"I wonder if the football players are feeling stressed or excited right now," Hailey commented.

"Probably excited. The adrenaline is going, and this is what they have been practicing for forever," Hope offered, based on her recent experience in the soccer state game.

"I'm so proud of all the players," Amanda gushed.

The girls grew quiet, and Amie could feel the tension in the air as Chelan lined up for the third and goal play.

Ben received the shotgun snap and started rolling to his right, looking for an open receiver. Just as two Lynden Christian players were closing in on Ben, he spotted Cody in the front of the end zone and fired a dart towards him. A Lynden Christian player got his hand on the ball just before it reached Cody, and the ball popped up in the air. The fans started to let out a groan when suddenly, out of nowhere, Ryan, who was running along the back of the end zone, reached out and grabbed the ball just before it hit the ground. The crowd roared with more decibels than ever! The girls were screaming Ryan's name and cheering loudly.

Chelan had scored with just three seconds remaining. After kicking the extra point and making a tackle on a short kickoff, time expired, and the celebration began.

The whole game, Amie had been longing for a hug from Josh, but he was sandwiched in the row behind her, so it wasn't too convenient to do anything but high five on the big plays. As soon as the last play ended, though, they both shoved their way to the aisle stairs to get to each other, and Josh picked her up with a huge hug and leaned in for a kiss. This was not what Amie expected, but, given the excitement of the moment, she was not disappointed.

Josh put his arm around her as he and the other guys talked about the game. Amie noticed that Conner had his arm around Hope as well. The area where they stood ended up being a cluster of fans as more and more of the Chelan crowd gathered around until someone yelled, "They're taking the picture!"

Everyone turned to see the players lined up with the seniors kneeling down in the front row, with Cody and Ryan holding the huge state trophy, and the other boys lined up standing in the back row. Everyone was snapping pictures from their phones while the official photographer got their shot down on the field.

The players were then shooed off the field because another two teams were about to have their division's Championship game. Amie and her friends rushed down the stairs and looked down from near the bottom of the stands to the concrete area to the left of the field, where the Chelan players were getting pictures with their friends and girlfriends. Someone quickly organized a shot of the senior players surrounded by Chelan's other senior students. Conner was down on the concrete in time to be included in the picture. There were several people who had made signs that made mention of the four football players who had died after the first scrimmage of the season. The team held one of the signs for another group picture and made the celebration even more memorable.

The coach and AD suggested that the fans move the celebration to the hotel lobby and wait for the players to arrive after they finish in the locker room. Amie turned to Josh and said, "See ya at the hotel celebration?"

I'll be there!" he promised. Amie smiled and then she and the other six girls hustled off to find their cars for the short ride back to the hotel.

This time, Hope, Amie, and Hailey were in the back seat of the SUV. Amie's cousin George couldn't quit talking about how he was definitely ready to be on the Chelan team when he became a freshman. The adults were rehashing the game as well, and there was a celebratory mood in the car.

When they got back to the hotel, the parking lot was already almost full, and Bob had to really look for a parking place. He dropped all his passengers at the glass sliding door while he found a spot to park. The girls burst into the lobby in force and commandeered a couch in the beautiful sitting area that was situated just past the front desk. The hotel was prepared for this celebration and were happy to accommodate them.

The celebration lasted about 90 minutes, with impromptu speeches and chances for fans to get pictures holding the mammoth trophy or standing with players. Hope saw Sierra and other members of her soccer team and went over to hug them, and Amie followed along with her. Both girls hugged Sierra, who clung tightly to the sign she had made honoring the players who had died earlier in the year, especially her boyfriend Bryan. Amie noticed a slight scent of alcohol on her breath.

"Bryan would have been so happy about this," Sierra reported. "He already knew this was going to happen. He talked about it all summer! He would have been proud. If only the soccer players had also won state!"

Hope agreed. "I wish we'd won for you seniors."

"Yeah, well, it was some of us seniors who ruined it for the team, so I guess we'll have to be satisfied with a second-place finish," she admitted ruefully.

"Second place is still pretty amazing!" Amie replied.

"We were lucky Hope moved to town," Sierra said, pointing toward Hope. "She was a key player." When Sierra leaned over and tossed an arm around both Hope and Amie for a picture one of her teammates was taking, Amie noticed alcohol on her breath again. She had also smelled the same scent on some of her other teammates. Amie could tell that Hope was glad that she had made the choice to spend the weekend with her instead of the soccer players.

Conner was catching a ride back to Chelan with another family, and they were taking off, so Hope and Amie went over to say goodbye to him.

Then, Josh said that he and Brett were heading back to campus. Amie was sad because she was hoping for another dinner like last weekend. He told her he'd call soon. She walked him to the sidewalk, and he gave her another kiss before he jogged off to catch up with Brett.

Amie and some of the other girls went shopping with Amie's mom and Aunt Debbie. Then, they had pizza in their rooms and went swimming in the hotel's pool.

****

The next morning, the two carloads went to a large church in Seattle that the girls had been wanting to visit. The music was great, and the message was Biblically sound and encouraging. The message referenced the book of Daniel from the Old Testament and what an effective leader Daniel turned out to be. They discussed how Daniel spent regular time with the Lord three times a day, and that was likely why he was so wise. Amie and the others in the group were inspired to carve out more time to be purposeful about their time with the Lord. Amie decided that if she ended up going to the University of Washington, she wanted this to be her church.

After the service was over, the group spent 45 minutes at Pike Place Market. The girls bought chocolate covered dried cherries that were delicious, and the moms each bought a beautiful bouquet of cut flowers. Amie's cousin George got a few wooden puzzle games, and Amie's dad purchased a cool hat.

As the girls settled in the back seat for their trip back to Chelan, Amie thought about how fortunate she was to have a family who were willing and able to drop everything to take her to the state tournament. She closed her eyes and prayed silently, thanking God for her wonderful family, the state tournament victory, her good friends, and the fact that she got to live in Chelan, a place that many other people only got to visit sometimes. She also thanked God for Josh, although she was disappointed that he didn't have much time for her.

She started to count her blessings and drifted off into a wonderful dreamland, filled with happy thoughts about the life she was so blessed to experience and the promise of more fun to come.

Books in The Guesthouse Girls Series

Summer Entanglements
Midsummer Adventures
Late Summer Love

Books in The Autumn Collection
Autumn of Kendi
Autumn of Hope
Autumn of Emma
Autumn of Amie

Upcoming books can be ordered, as they
are released, through
Amazon.

Please engage with us on social media!
Facebook: The Guesthouse Girls
(@theguesthousegirlsbooks)
Instagram: @judyannkoglin_author

Acknowledgements

Autumn of Amie is the seventh book in The Guesthouse Girls series and probably the last for the time being. Amie's book was perhaps a bit more intense than the others, but I felt that it was important to share a variety of experiences and emotions that girls sometimes face. As always, I want to send out a shout-out to my faithful proofreaders: Kay, Kathy, and Wade Koglin; my editor, Savannah Cottrell, @thewonderedits; my illustrator Angie @coldgigie, my supportive digital marketing coach, Liza @amauiblog, and my cover designer, Joanna Alonzo. Special thanks to my daughter-in-law Lauren, a nurse, who helped me with the section about Grandpa Peterson, and Jeremy Weber who gave me some background on the town of Waterville. God led me through this whole process and I trust that He will put these stories into the hands that need to read them!

Author

Judy Ann Koglin is an author of young adult Christian fiction. She lived most of her life in Washington State and spent several fun vacations in Chelan. She and her husband Wade currently live on the island of Maui. Together, they are the proud parents of two boys, Tyler and Tim, and a daughter in-law Lauren.

Printed in Great Britain
by Amazon

77745939R00133